Breath of Life

(Soul Collectors)

A novel by

Deanna Breen

Chapter 1

Hit and Run

Rayne was sitting in her living room with her parents while the news was on the television. She watched as a teacher from her school flashed across the screen. The report was stating that he had been arrested for misconduct with some students at Rayne's high school. The teacher also possessed of a stash of child pornography. The report stated that after he posted bail, he was found dead in his driveway and that an autopsy would be performed in order to establish cause of death.

Rayne was in shock, particularly because Mr. Jones was one of her favorite teachers. She was disappointed at what the news was reporting and stared in disbelief. Towards the end of the report her phone rang and she could see it was her friend Lydia. Rayne dismissed Lydia's first call but she was persistent. Lydia called back two more times before Rayne answered hesitantly. She was engrossed with the story on her television. "Hi Lydia."

Lydia was slow to respond. When she did her voice was hushed. "Hi Rayne, can you talk?" Lydia sounded almost like she was crying.

"Sure, what's up? Is everything okay?" Rayne walked back to her room to take the call. Lydia was still quiet, almost cryptic. "Rayne, have you seen the news?"

Lydia was a classmate. She did not have many friends, but she and Rayne had gone to school together since kindergarten. Lydia confided in Rayne often. Rayne responded to her question. "Do you mean about Mr. Jones? I was watching it before you called. Can you believe it? It's total crap, he was the best teacher! I can't believe he did it! I can't believe he's gone."

Lydia stayed quiet causing Rayne to get impatient. "Lydia, that is what you mean right? Are you there?" Lydia was soft when she spoke and still sounded like she was crying. "Rayne, it's true. It did happen, but not like the news is saying. It was only one student, me."

Rayne was stunned and hesitated before she responded. She could not believe it. Lydia had never been a liar or the kind of student that would have a relationship with a teacher. "No way Lydia! How could this be? When did it happen? You and Mr. Jones, how?" Rayne was trying to understand how a teacher could find any interest in a student. She had heard about it before at other schools, but never imagined it would happen at her school, to a friend and a teacher she admired. Lydia choked up as she spoke, "I don't know what to do Rayne." Rayne was struggling to find the words to console Lydia.

"Are you going to school tomorrow? What are your parents doing about it?" Rayne wanted to help her friend and now she was getting upset thinking about Mr. Jones. She could not believe he would do anything with a student but she believed Lydia. "My parents know. They are obviously mad. I have to go to school tomorrow because I have to talk to the principal. They are going to make me take home studies for a few weeks." Lydia had stopped crying.

"Oh that sucks. Is there anything I can do for you?" Rayne felt bad for her friend. Lydia was grateful, "No, I just needed someone to talk to. Thank you Rayne. Oh, and please don't tell anyone." Rayne was good with secrets, even one as scandalous as this. "Don't worry I won't. You're welcome."

Rayne went back into the living room with her parents. The television was off and her dad was reading the newspaper aloud. "This winter is projected to be a cold one for Southern California and its unsuspecting residents." He also referred to the recent accident that happened on the route Rayne would be taking later that day. The final quote her dad read from the local news was about a police officer that was up on charges for aggravated rape. "Sometimes it's like we don't know who to trust these days." Tom shook his head in disgust.

Rayne could not agree more after learning about her friend and her teacher. She wanted to forget the bad news in the world and focus on something more positive. Rayne was involved with a student church group that delivered donated blankets and coats collected by the church. The horrible news provoked Rayne to work longer handing them to the homeless in her area that evening.

She had been helping the community for many years. Now that she was in her senior year of high school, her parents had been giving her and her friend Sarah more freedom to do unsupervised deliveries. There was always a risk helping street people. Rayne and Sarah's parents mandated some safety precautions they were required to fulfill before they went out on their own. They both had to take a self-defense class, carry their cell phones, and check in frequently while they were out. They were delivering within less than five miles of where Rayne lived, Lakeland Village. It was a hotspot for vagrants. The population was blended from middle-class to the destitute.

Rayne usually worked until dusk for safety reasons. The area was both suburban and rural but busy. It did not have many street lights or sidewalks. The excuse the city gave for limited lighting was light pollution competing with local astrologers. Grand Avenue was a heavily traveled street and frequently, pedestrians would become a tragic news story. With no real sidewalks, people would have to walk along the street side playing an unintentional game of road chicken.

When Rayne picked up Sarah, she was partially distracted by her conversation with Lydia. "Hey Rayne, did you see the news about Mr. Jones?" Sarah was out of breath as she hopped into Rayne's car. Rayne wanted to answer but simply nodded her head yes. "I just can't believe it! Mr. Jones was one of my favorite teachers. I wonder who the students are." Sarah's curiosity was wearing on Rayne so she just shrugged her shoulders and ended the conversation.

Knowing the temperature was reported to drop to near freezing before the week was over, Rayne had felt the pressing obligation to ensure some kind of comfort for those who could not afford to supply their own. At the church, she and Sarah loaded her Honda CRV and set off for deliveries. She parked on side streets and at one stop, the girls walked as far as a quarter mile before they went back to move the car and supply the next point. The work was a good distraction for Rayne. She was genuinely disgusted for knowing about Mr. Jones and Lydia, and she was confused about how to feel about him dyeing.

By the time of their fourth drop-off, the evening sky was fading from azure blue to sapphire. Sarah was having a hard time warming up from their last delivery so Rayne told her to stay in the car because it was their last stop and she felt they were at a safe area.

She had gathered as many blankets as her arms could hold along with a few jackets. The site she headed toward was three-hundred yards from the car. Rayne knew there would be a small group that she had met during the summer when she was passing out water. She had gotten ten feet from where the group usually gathered when suddenly she was slammed to the ground and everything went dark.

As she lay on the frigid ground, a sensation of extreme cold overtook her quickly then a comforting warmth blanketed her. She was unsure of what she was sensing or seeing. She had a surreal feeling that she was picked up into someone's arms and was being carried somewhere. She had been plunged into lucid dreams. She felt as though she was flying when abruptly a rush of anger exploded in her. She was confused about what was happening and fought to open her eyes. As she remained in limbo, an evil jolt hit her before a peaceful feeling of warmth came over her again. In her sub-conscience state, a camp fire appeared then the excitement of dancing freely lifted her. Years seemed to pass in minutes. Her sleep brought sights of places she had never seen. Then suddenly nothing and everything was black.

In the distance she could hear her parents' voice, "She is trying to open her eyes." Rayne did not know what was going on or where she was? Her eyes fluttered then finally opened completely, squinting to focus.

"Honey don't talk. Everything is going to be okay now." Both of her parents were holding her hands and looked relieved. Rayne could hear a heart monitor and saw that she had an I.V. in her arm. There was a doctor in the room. She was confused and did not know why she was in a hospital room. As she tried to swallow she winced. Then she noticed her throat was sore and her lungs felt heavy. She could not remember what had happened to put her in the hospital bed. She tried to talk but did not have the energy to push out the words. "Sweetie, please save your strength." Her mom's voice was kind and reassuring.

Rayne was quickly exhausted and dozed off. The next time she woke her parents were sleeping in the chairs next to her bed. Finally, she was able to mumble the word "mom". Janie's eyes opened and she smiled at her daughter.

"How are you?"

Rayne stuttered as she spoke, "Mom, why am I here?"

"Someone brought you here. You don't remember what happened?"

"No… Sarah." Rayne realized she had left her friend behind.

"Sarah is okay. She was in the car waiting for you but you never came back. That's when she heard the accident happen and you disappeared."

"Accident?" Rayne was puzzled and completely foggy about an accident.

"Yes. One of the people you were trying to help was hit by a car. Sarah heard the impact and thought it was you. She'd gone over to see if you were okay but you weren't there. All that was left was the homeless man in the street and the car that stopped after it struck the man. The driver said he never saw a girl, just the man that leapt in front of his car."

"Where is he? The homeless man." Rayne was still staggering as she spoke.

"Sweetie, he didn't make it. They said he didn't suffer. The impact… it was hard. He passed instantly."

"Mom, I don't remember." It was harder for her speak now because she had a knot in her throat feeling pain for the person who died. A tear rolled down the top of her cheek, her mother wiped it and kissed her forehead.

"How long have I been here?"

"We were so worried we would never see you again. You disappeared for a day, then a Good Samaritan brought you here and left without leaving a name. There isn't even a description of the person, only that he was a young man. You've been here for five days... sleeping and mumbling. Or trying to mumble."

"I think I'm hungry."

"The doctor said you can start with ice chips then liquid. He also reminded me that you'll have to take it slowly. I'll get the nurse to bring you some."

"What time is it?"

"Midnight." Her dad, exhausted from worry, unintentionally slept through his wife and daughter's conversation. "Tom, Rayne is awake." He sat up quickly and smiled at her, "good morning my sweet angel." Tom's voice was just as soothing as Janie's. Rayne liked to see her dad smile. "Tom, stay with Rayne while I get the nurse to find some ice chips for her." Janie left and Tom held his daughter's hand.

"Sorry dad." Rayne was genuinely remorse for the man that died and for worrying her parents.

"For what? You were just trying to help those people. You have nothing to be sorry about."

"Sorry for worrying you."

"Don't be silly. Worrying is a parent's job. You're okay now and that's all that matters."

Rayne dozed off again. Her mom came in with the ice chips but did not want to wake her. Rayne slept and dreamt all night. In her dreams she felt the anger come again. She woke to her mom's voice, "Rayne, Rayne, are you okay?"

"Yeah mom, what's wrong?"

"I think you were dreaming. You were growling or something. Maybe moaning or yelling. I couldn't tell but you didn't seem happy."

"I don't remember it. It definitely must have been a dream. I was really growling? So when do I get to go home?"

"Now there is the Rayne I know. Yes you were growling or what sounded like growling. The doctor thinks one more day will be good. How do you feel?" Janie was happy Rayne was sounding like herself again.

"Better I guess. Can I start to walk?"

"I'll ask the doctor." Janie left the room and quickly returned with him.

Dr. Jones followed Janie into the room. "So you think you are ready to walk? I guess we could try, nothing seems to be wrong with your legs or spine."

"Spine? What would be wrong with my spine?" Rayne looked puzzled when she questioned the doctor about her spine.

"We weren't sure if you were part of the accident so you've had an MRI. Nothing is broken, as a matter of fact we can't find anything wrong with you except for some irritation in your lungs and esophagus. We want to watch you for one more day to see if anything surfaces but you seem to be fit-as-a-fiddle." The doctor appeared upbeat about Rayne's condition.

"So I can try to walk now?"

"Let's get you sitting up first." The doctor and nurse helped her to move slowly. She sat up then they put down the bars on her bed so she could swing her legs over. She felt dizzy sitting up and her feet tingled when they dangled off of the side of the bed.

"How does that feel?" Dr. Jones asked.

"Dizzy, tingly but I am okay."

"Okay we'll do this a few times before we let you walk. When we know you can stand, we'll disconnect some of these devices."

"The sooner the better." Rayne sounded frustrated when she spoke about getting out of bed.

"Don't rush. You don't want to cause unnecessary injury just to have to stay here longer do you?" The doctor rubbed her arm to comfort her as he spoke. She nodded in agreement with her physician.

The little bit of physical activity exhausted Rayne enough to put her to sleep again. Her dreams were the same, but this time the dancing came back. She smiled as she seemed to float around the fire listening to sounds of joy from other dancers. Her sleep was short and when she awoke, she was alone in the room. She sat up by herself and managed to reach for the cup on her medicine table. She did not realize how thirsty she was until she emptied her cup.

Just as she set the cup back down, the doctor came in and told her it was time to walk. While gripping onto the nurse and her mom, she lifted herself to her feet. The blood rushed making her feel light headed but she did not let them know. She stood for a minute then put a foot forward. After a few minutes she was across the room and she moved a little faster when she headed back to her bed.

"Looks good. We will have you do that for the rest of the day and by tonight we can take off most of your monitors."

Janie hugged her and helped her lay down. "You look tired, try to rest again."

"Thank you mom." With that, Rayne was asleep again. Her naps were short and frequent but full of dreams. Each time she woke up her mom helped her to walk until she started to walk on her own.

The next morning Dr. Jones came in with the good news that Rayne was going home. "Thank goodness!" Rayne exclaimed before he could finish his thought.

"Come on Rayne, this place isn't so bad. At least you got to catch up on your rest."

"No it isn't bad at all but I would've rather not been here." Rayne gave a joking scowl then the doctor shot her a grin and a wink.

He signed the paper for discharge and they went to the nurse's station to check out. The nurse on duty asked about the young man that had come to visit the evening before. Janie said she did not know about a visitor and that no one had gone into Rayne's room. The nurse just shrugged it off, but it was now a seed planted in Rayne's head. While she was curious about her visitor, she was more anxious to leave the hospital.

Chapter 2

Home

A welcome home banner hung on her house over the door. Sarah and her parents were inside when they walked in. When Sarah saw Rayne, she burst into tears and ran to hug her. "Oh Rayne, I am so sorry. I should have never let you go alone!"

"Sarah, it's okay. I am fine now. Did you get the rest of the blankets out?"

A laughing sob came out of Sarah "Rayne don't be silly. You were more important. We started looking for you so the blankets had to wait." They all laughed because it was typical of Rayne, which is why she got hurt in the first place. Everyone in the room took a turn hugging her before they went to the living room to talk about the week and how well Rayne looked.

"There posters of you put up all over the school."

Rayne rolled her eyes as she responded with sarcasm. "Great, I go all these years being unnoticed and now I am the talk of the town."

"You made the Patch too. You were their top story, you even trumped the story about Mr. Jones. Oh, and wait until I tell you the students that were involved!" Sarah had a perplexed smile when she told Rayne about being a story in the local online news source and Sarah's mom had hushed her about the student teacher story. Rayne had completely forgot about Lydia and Mr. Jones. "I think I need to rest." Rayne looked depleted when she spoke, then she sighed and plopped onto the couch.

Janie used her charming disposition to affectionately excuse Rayne and suggest a later visit. The group left with some final well wishes before Rayne went to her room. She collapsed on her bed and found sleep quickly. The dreams started immediately. She could feel her breath being sucked out of her as she looked into dark eyes. Time stopped. While still in her dream, she was in a room that flickered with candlelight. In the room there was a coyote and a crow. They were looking at her as she lay warm under covers, then everything went black. Suddenly, she was dancing around the fire feeling joy through the beat of drums.

Rayne woke up quickly when the bedroom door creaked as it opened. Her mom peaked in and asked how she was doing.

"Good mom, thank you. When is dinner?"

"We've been waiting for you to get up. Are you hungry?"

"Starving. I'll be ready in a few minutes."

A feast was set at the table. It looked as if Janie made all of Rayne's favorites. They said their dinner blessing and made their plates. It had been almost two weeks since she had a home cooked meal and Rayne managed to eat three plates full. "I am glad to see you have an appetite, plus some. Wow Rayne, I don't think you've ever eaten so much."

"It can't possibly be that I missed your food mom? Thank you, it was delicious. I think I'm gonna go for a walk now. I kind of need to get out and stretch my legs." Rayne did miss her mother's meals but there was something different that made her feel famished.

"Do you want us to go with you or maybe you could bring a friend?"

"Mom, I'll be fine. I want to be by myself anyway."

"Please stay close and keep your phone on you."

"Will do. Don't worry, I'll stay close."

Janie knew she could not keep Rayne locked up and protected forever. She watched as her daughter strolled down the street. Their housing area had two entry points and was, for the most part, enclosed creating a certain sense of false safety.

As Rayne walked she managed to find herself in a day dream. She was behind the eyes of something that was breathless and appeared to be stalking someone. The eyes seemed to be confused and almost frustrated. Not realizing she was headed toward the main street, the sound of a car horn jarred her from her trance. Breathing heavy, she tried to make sense of her walking dream. She did not remember walking to the spot where she stood.

Although she was compelled to go further along the main intersection, she forced herself to head back home. Inside the house her mom questioned where she had gone and if she paid attention to her text. Unintentionally, she ignored her mom and walked toward her room. "Rayne, did you hear me? Are you okay? Did you read your text?"

"Oh hey mom, I'm fine just a little distracted. No. I didn't hear my phone. Sorry. I'm going to bed early tonight if we don't have anything going on." It was Saturday and usually Rayne liked to stay up and read.

"Please don't scare me like that again, I was worried. I think going to bed early is probably a good idea." Janie hugged Rayne before she went off to her room.

In her bedroom she sat by the window. It was early evening and already frigid outside, but she wanted to feel the air so she slid her window open. She looked at the sparse stars that sprinkled the twilight sky while she listened intently to the sounds of night. She could hear the neighborhood dogs bark as a lone coyote howled. She tuned into the sound of the coyote. It seemed like it was calling to something.

Rayne fell asleep with the window open. Her dreams were wild and vivid, but were broken when her mom entered the room protesting to having the window open with what felt like freezing temperatures. Janie felt Rayne's cheeks to make sure she was not feverish. After the confirmation of good health and closing the window, she left Rayne to sleep.

The rest of her night was a dreamless sleep and she awoke feeling lost. The dreams she had been having where a comfort to her. Dreamless sleep caused Rayne to act a little more out of character. She had snapped at her mom during breakfast and she chose to stay home while her parents went to Sunday services. They had been going to church since Rayne could remember but that morning she did not want to go. All she wanted to do was go back to sleep to see if she could find her dreams.

Hesitant to leave her alone, Janie and Tom went about their normal routine and Rayne went back to bed. In her sleep, she sensed something bad. She could feel herself standing near someone but she could not see a physical presence. She could feel what they were thinking and did not like the perversion of her horrible dream companions. Her sub-conscience urge to attack that person was overwhelming and suddenly she was unable to breathe. She woke coughing and choking for air. This was a nightmare and it did not give her the answers nor comfort she was looking for. She was grateful it was merely a bad dream.

When she found her breath she sat up and looked out at the clear sky. Her stomach was growling with hunger pangs so she went to the kitchen to rummage some leftover breakfast. Her parents came in just as she reheated her food.

"Are you feeling better Rayne?"

"Yeah mom, sorry for this morning. I was just real tired, now I am starving. How was church?"

"It was good. Everyone asked about you. I'm glad you're feeling better."

"Me too. Now I'm just gonna clean out the fridge."

"That's good, you need to eat. Waste-not want-not."

Rayne finished her food and went to get cleaned up for the day. She wanted to go for a drive. She told her parents she would be gone for about an hour or two but she would make sure to keep her cell on. When she got in her car she did not know where she planned on going, so she drove. She found herself driving toward the forest that was miles from her house. It was part of the Ortega Highway. It was a beautifully treacherous drive.

A site to the right of the road was open for hikers to park. She pulled into a spot and turned her car off. There was no one around and the silence was heavy. She got out of her car and was quickly on a path. She came to a clearing that appeared to have had a fire ring and there were a few crows perched on the tree branches above her. They seemed to be following her as she walked. She circled the fire ring as the birds watched.

The only sound she could hear were her footsteps and pinecones falling. Suddenly there was a snap, as if someone stepped on a stick. Rayne froze and looked up in the direction of the sound but saw nothing. She felt compelled to walk toward what she had heard and kept her eyes focused on the spot. The birds' eyes followed her. Rayne used her hand to move shrubs out of her way. She could see broken branches leading to a side path, which was the direction she decided to go.

Following deeper into the woods she moved steadily, hearing another crack. The trees were getting dense and she finally felt a sense of fear. Walking a few more steps she jumped back as a coyote leapt in front of her. She lost her breath and fell to the ground. Using her hands to brace her fall, she had scratched up both palms. Keeping her eyes on the coyote, she slowly stood up. For a second she glanced to see the crows then drew her eyes back to the coyote. It gave her one warning growl then darted off into the brush.

The sound in the woods stopped. Without warning the crows took flight into the sky through the trees. As a sense of emptiness came over Rayne, an impending need to be in her car pushed her to go back.

It was difficult to navigate her way back because she had not realized she had gone so deep into the forest. She was frazzled when she finally found the fire ring that led to the path that took her to her car. As she approached her car door, her cell phone pinged a text. Before she pulled away from her parking spot she stopped to respond. It was her mom and Rayne did not want to worry her anymore. While she was typing the letters into her cell something caught her eye along the tree line. She peered into the eyes of the coyote. A shiver went up her spine as she drove off.

The location where the accident had happened was along her drive home. Out of morbid curiosity, she wanted to stop to check it out. It was difficult to pull over because the space was narrow but she found a little outlet to stop at. She put her hazard lights on and got out to survey the area. This was a common spot for her to drive past. It was bright out and the events of the night and of the accident were difficult to recall in the sunlight.

Rayne remembered walking with her hands full and hearing laughter from the group she was heading toward. She found her way to the spot where everything went black. The road still had the markings from the accident and the spot where the homeless man had died. In a brief second she had thought of her own mortality and how she could be dead rather than the homeless man. Struggling to remember what happened, Rayne frustrated herself and decided to go home.

Walking back to her car, she found herself taking deep breaths. Again, something caught her attention through the corner of her eye. It was the coyote, stealth along the tree line.

She looked up at the electrical lines and there were the crows looking down on her. Still breathing deeply, she sped up to her car. Confused by what was happening, she needed a distraction. She turned on her radio, popped in a Mumford & Sons CD, and hurried home.

Chapter 3

School

Monday morning came early and for the first time since childhood, Rayne was not overly excited to go to school. During the night, her dreams were confusing, the coyote followed her, and the crows kept watch. She wanted to dance and feel joy in her dream but the dance never came. Breakfast was quiet. Sarah came knocking at the door and broke the silence. Rayne was her ride to school. "Good morning. Are you ready?"

"Hold on. Let me get my books and say goodbye."

"Bye mom and dad. I'm going to the library after school today so I'll be a little late. Love you."

"Be careful and have fun at school. Text me when you get to the library. Love you."

During the drive to school Sarah started to probe her. "Are you nervous about going back? How are you feeling? Do you remember anything? Wait till you see everyone at school. You're a star there now. It's crazy how everyone has come together."

"Sarah, I'm not nervous. I feel fine and I don't remember anything. As a matter of fact, I tried to remember yesterday when I went back to where the accident was but I can't remember a thing. I'm not interested in all the attention and honestly, I really don't want to go back to school."

"Sorry Rayne. It'll be okay. I'll help you. Whatever you need let me know."

"Thank you Sarah." Rayne felt bad for lashing out at Sarah.

Welcome back signs were everywhere. There were crowds of students gathering around when Rayne walked up. They were all cheering her on and reaching out to try to touch her. It was loud and uncomfortable when the principal finally got to her and helped her through to the office. "Sorry about that Rayne. Everyone is just so excited to see that you are alright."

"That's okay as long as they all get over it and things go back to normal."

"I'm sure it will. Let me know if you need anything."

"Thank you Mr. Smith. I don't want to be late for class." There was a small crowd outside the office that gathered and walked with her to class. She could not hear what everyone was saying because it was a loud mess.

Rayne caught up with Lydia during lunch. They talked about what happened before Rayne was hurt. "You know when they found him dead they couldn't understand what had killed him. They said it looked like natural causes, maybe a heart attack. He was too young to have a heart attack, right? There were rumors that they did something to him when he was in jail. Rayne, he was seeing another student. That's what got him into trouble. Her parents found out when they looked at her cell phone. After they reported it, the police went through Mr. Jones' cell phone and found pictures and texts from me. Rayne I'm so sorry that you were hurt but one good thing did come out of it, everyone forgot about me." Lydia hugged Rayne.

Throughout the day the insanity calmed down and by the end of the day, things were nearly normal. Rayne and Sarah managed to get to the car without incident. "Do you want to go to the library with me?" Rayne wanted to get some homework done and she always liked working in the library.

"Sure, what's going on there?"

"I just don't feel like being home so I thought I would do my homework there."

"Okay sounds good. Let me text my mom, I'm sure she'll say yes." Sarah felt like she needed to keep an eye on Rayne so she asked her mom if she could go to the library.

The parking lot had few cars in it so the girls parked close to the door. As they entered Rayne started to breathe heavily. Sarah noticed it, "Are you okay?"

"Yeah, why?"

"You are breathing real loud and we've barely walked."

"I didn't notice." Still laboring with her breath, she made her way to the seats by the periodicals. She sat with her books and pulled open a folder. "Sarah, does it feel... weird...?"

"What do you mean weird?"

"Don't know. Can't explain it," she whispered. She looked down at her folder but was suddenly drawn to look up and as she did she caught a glimpse of the eyes. He was peeking around the newspaper he was reading and his eyes were as black as coal. She recognized the eyes and her skin bumped while her breathing stopped. "Sarah, let's go."

"Why? What's wrong? We just got here."

"Just get up. Let's go" she said gathering her things and pulling Sarah out of the library. Outside the crows were lined on the rooftop watching as the two climbed into the car. Rayne screeched her tires when she pulled out of the parking lot.

"Rayne, what's wrong?"

"My mom text me and wants me home," was all Rayne could think to say. In reality she did not know why she wanted to get out of there so quickly.

"Okay well you didn't have to try to pull my arm out of my socket to get my attention."

"Sorry. I just don't want to worry my mom you know." Rayne dropped Sarah off in a hurry then rushed to her house. She walked in quickly and accidently closed the door too hard. Janie was home from work early "Rayne is that you? I thought you were at the library. Why did you slam the door?"

"Sorry mom, the door slipped. The library was too crowded, I'm fine." Rayne was looking forward to the day when everyone would stop asking her how she was doing or how she was feeling. She did not welcome the attention and could not explain how she we feeling. She wanted life to get back to normal but normal seemed so far away.

She could not figure out what it was it about the library or why the boy with the dark eyes had startled her. She had never seen him before but she acknowledged his eyes to be as familiar as her dreams. The way he looked at her was penetrating. In the same instant, the coyote and crows were equally disarming.

Keeping things to herself had become a new routine for Rayne. Hiding what she knew about Lydia and Mr. Jones and now her paranoid private life. She had no one to confide in because she knew all the strangeness of the situation would sound crazy and irrational. She had hoped she was imagining it all. Maybe it was due her injuries during her accident. She had to force herself to stop thinking about it.

At dinner her mom asked her about her day. Rayne was animated as she gave an almost exaggerated description about the school drama. She had hoped it would appease her mom. Her dad laughed as he listened. He knew about his daughter's discomfort with attention and appreciated her attempt at tolerance with a crowd. Rayne had not been overly spirited since she had been home and this show of entertainment was a reassuring sign for her parents.

After two full plates of dinner Rayne helped with the dishes. Once she was done she excused herself to finish her homework. She mentioned to her mom that she had serious catching up to do.

In her room she could see outside while she sat at her desk. The sun was lowering and the sky looked like watercolor. She was distracted by the view until she noticed another crow perched on a tree by her house. The crow looked like it was looking in but Rayne worked to convince herself that it was a just a strange coincidence. She dredged through her distractions and completed her homework until it was time for a shower and bed.

Rayne's night was a busy flurry of dreams. She was walking through the forest where she had hiked once before in a dream, only this time she went further in. She followed the coyote and came upon makeshift tents and clothes on a line. The camp was empty but the crows were around and there were more coyotes. The sky dimmed from light to dark and she became trapped, contained by lack of movement. The eyes came in and circled her. She could feel them on her back and she shivered. There was a tickle on her arm and a whisper of air on the nape of her neck but still, she could not move. A strong breeze blew and the crows and coyotes dispersed. She had gone from feeling warm and tickled to freezing and scared. Gasping for air, she shook herself awake. As she sat up in her bed she had noticed she was breathing deeply. She woke up minutes before her alarm sounded and was relieved to find the whole night was a dream.

Shaken from what she had seen in her dream, Rayne sat a minute to compose herself. Noticing that she had lost ten minutes sitting in a blank stare, she had to rush getting ready for school. She gathered her books and went to the kitchen for breakfast. Janie was waiting in the kitchen appearing as if she wanted to talk, but Rayne made short of any conversation. She sped out the door with a hurried goodbye.

In front of Sarah's, house Rayne sat in the car and honked her horn. Sarah was sliding her coat on as she closed her house door. "Why are you so early?"

"It's only a few minutes early and I'm hoping that I can avoid the 'welcome' crowd." She felt a deeper urge to get to school early but could not articulate it.

As the two drove their usual route, they passed a group of kids. In the morning it would be common for any group of kids to be walking to school together, but Rayne was intently drawn to focus on this particular group. Not noticing she had slowed her speed, she managed to fix her eyes on the boy; those eyes of coal piercing into hers. She started to breathe heavily again and a horn honked behind her. "Rayne, are you okay? Why are you going so slow, do you know them?"

"Oh crap, I didn't realize my speed. No, I don't know them. One just looked familiar. They don't go to our school, do they?"

"I don't recognize any of them."

"Yeah, you're right. I think I might have seen one of them in the library."

"Could be. Now will you get us to school safely? I thought you were trying to avoid the crowd and driving this slow is going to land you right in the middle of the chaos."

That morning during the video announcements, Rayne saw her picture with an article submitted by The Patch about her first day back at school. She did not have to deal with the crowd but seeing herself on the television was equally humiliating. She was over all of the attention.

The rest of the day was uneventful until the drive home. Rayne was getting used to having the crows around but there seemed to be an uncomfortable number of them lined up on the wire above the school parking lot. The girls got in the car and as they drove out of the school parking lot, the dark haired group of kids were gathered again across the street. Rayne's eyes fixed on his eyes once more when all the crows flew off the fence line. Sarah was startled by the birds "Oh… what the? Where did they come from? Do you see that? Look at all of them!"

"What? The birds? Yeah, I've noticed them lately." Rayne could feel him staring at her car until she was out of sight.

She dropped Sarah off and when she went into her house, her mom stopped her before she went into her room to work. "Hi Rayne. How was your day?"

"Good mom. Going to do homework now."

"When you're done will you do me a favor? I need a few things from the grocery store and I am in the middle of a report. Can you go for me?"

"Sure. I don't have much homework today anyway."

Before the accident, Rayne always went to the store for her mom. She liked to go because it was Janie's sneaky way of giving Rayne extra money. Janie let her keep the change as kind of a reward for helping out. At the market, Rayne picked up everything on the list and went to check out. After she put what she had needed on the counter, she looked down into her purse to get the money. Just as she looked up to the greeting from the checker, she froze. There *he* was, bagging her groceries. The tall boy was looking at her with his dark eyes. She was flushed and suddenly stumbling to find a response to the checkers greeting. The boy's eyes did not leave her as he asked, "do you need help out?" His voice was deep and hearing him made her cheeks flash a deeper shade of red. "No…thank…you" she managed to squeak before she thanked the checker.

Feeling rattled and dizzy, she rushed to her car and fumbled with her car keys. Losing grip of them, they dropped to the ground. She bent to pick them up the same time his large hand reached for them "Let me get those for you". Her mouth went dry and her blood pulsed. Rayne's manners escaped her and in her disarray, she could not even mutter the words 'thank you'. "I just came out to get carts. Can I take yours for you?" She took her groceries and stepped away from the cart. Still, she did not say thank you. He smiled showing his perfectly brilliant white teeth and somehow there was a twinkle in his eyes of coal. "Have a nice day."

He pushed the cart away and she got in her car. It was the first time he had broken his gaze on her before she did. He stopped at the curb with the other carts and watched as she left the parking lot. On the drive home she found herself thinking about him. She did not know his name but she knew his smile.

Inside the house her mom helped put the groceries away and noticed Rayne looking distant, "Hey, are you in there Rayne?"

"Sorry mom, just thinking about homework." What Rayne was actually thinking was, it was strange how she felt being around that boy. She was not herself in his presence, but suddenly had a comforting pull toward him. When he stood next to her, she did not feel broken. Her new reality was, being in the house she had grown up in and known her entire life, she felt alone. She was confused and trying to understand why she sensed she was missing a part of something.

Chapter 4

Searching

Saturday morning Rayne took Sarah hiking. Janie did not want Rayne to go alone so it took a bit of convincing to get Sarah to agree on the trip. She had not told Sarah anything about the boy and was not sure if she ever would. On their way out, Rayne wanted to stop at the store and pick up snacks. She went to the same grocery store she knew he worked at. Inside, the store was quiet and too early for many shoppers. The girls picked up trail mix, water, string cheese and fruit. Rayne could not see him anywhere but she could sense him.

After concluding he probably would not surface, she steered Sarah through the fast check-out. The two were chatting as they rounded the corner to the car. Rayne did not have to look up to know he was standing by her car. Sarah saw Rayne's face and looked in the same direction, "What's he doing here?"

"It looks like he works here." The girls walked closer to the car and chatted as they attempted to ignore his stare.

"Hi Rayne." His tone was even.

"Hi." She did not think of the fact that he knew her name but she was finally able to struggle through her confused senses and respond.

"Where are you heading out to today?" He was making small talk.

"Hiking." Rayne did not look up as she spoke

"Just the two of you? Are you staying local?"

Sarah chimed in because she did not like his inquisition, "Yes the two of us and what does it matter if it's local?"

While he ignored Sarah's question, he smugly directed his attention to her and reciprocated in her same tone. "Hi, I'm Caleb and you are?"

"Sarah, since you feel it's your business. Speaking of your business, shouldn't you be collecting carts or bagging groceries or something?"

"Yeah, I'll get right to it. Be careful out there. It isn't safe for girls to be venturing into the woods alone." He moved out of their way and the girls got in the car.

"What a creep! And did you see his eyes? No color. Do you think they were contacts? Not to mention those horrible crows! They're everywhere these days!" Sarah protested the whole scene.

By now, Rayne had noticed the crows less and Caleb more. All Rayne could think was that she finally knew his name, Caleb.

As they pulled onto Grand Avenue Sarah was reminded of a recent death. "Oh hey did you see the news? Another accident on Grand. They say the guy was riding his bicycle drunk and drove out in front of a car. They seriously need to put in more street lights and maybe a sidewalk."

"Well maybe if people learned to behave themselves they wouldn't get hurt. Sometimes being dumb just gets you killed." Rayne was developing a lack of tolerance for malicious and ignorant behavior. She was losing empathy.

"Wow Rayne! When did you get so dark? You're usually the nice one of the two of us. You sound so cynical with that statement, like an overly opinionated politician. The man was just drinking and riding." Sarah was really surprised by Rayne's comment.

"Well you know some people can't change their wayward ways so they get them changed for them. It seems like checks and balances to me."

"Hello, earth to Rayne. Seriously, what's happened to you?"

"Nothing, I was just thinking out loud." That was the end of Rayne's rant.

There were no cars parked for hiking. The girls were early and it appeared that they beat the other nature enthusiast up the hill. Rayne led Sarah on the path she had gone on before.

She wanted to see if the tents in her dream existed. The path was a little more worn but if she had not been on it before she would have missed it. The crows were scattered through the trees and Rayne was the only one who noticed them. Sarah trotted clumsily and was trying to pay attention to where she was walking. Finally, after a few bends along the path, they came to a clearing. It was open and had a small fire pit.

Rayne sensed that something had been there. It was the exact spot in her dream, only now it was empty. Sarah asked her what she was looking for. "Nothing, I just feel like I know this spot. Have you ever felt like that before? Do you want to have our snack here?"

"Sure. It seems nice enough and I think you mean is 'Deja vu'." Sarah pulled her small backpack off and sat on a tree trunk. The two took some time to engage in small talk and listen to the sounds of the forest. Ten minutes into their break, they heard a crack along the tree line. A coyote emerged and looked at the two with its head dropped low. As it stood still they heard another crack behind the coyote. The girls were startled when a tall figure walked up to the animal. It was Caleb and his eyes immediately focused on Rayne's "I told you, it isn't safe for you girls to be out here alone. Does anyone know where you are?"

The girls both looked at each other in panic. Rayne was the first to speak up "It's perfectly safe for us if we know how to defend ourselves." She made sure to appear confident but inside she was trembling. "Besides, we have friends meeting up with us in a bit." Rayne lied but in her panic, it was the only thing she could think of. No one was coming. Rayne had become an expert at quick thinking now that she was a constant secret keeper. Sarah was at a complete loss for words, she could only mumble a broken sentence, "yeah, waiting for friends".

"How do you know about this place?" Caleb's tone was accusatory.

"It is a public hiking area, most of the hikers out here know about this place. We didn't know about it, but how hard is it to follow a path. How do you know about it… and weren't you just at work?" Rayne was defensive and accusatory at the same time.

"That isn't an easy path to follow. I know because I am the one who made it and I don't know of any hikers coming this way. I worked early and was just about to get off when you two were at the store. Who are you meeting up here?"

"Just friends, why?" Rayne made sure to seem matter-of-factly.

"Curious." Caleb responded dismissively.

"Well since they aren't here yet I am guessing they got lost so we are going to head back down now before they send a search party." Rayne spoke confidently.

"Probably a good idea. Do you want me to walk with you?"

"No, I think we can manage." For a moment she lost her temper with Caleb and became curt with him.

"Please be careful and holler if you need me. I'll be sticking around here for a bit. Oh, and sorry if I scared you."

"Are you waiting for someone?"

"No, I just come here for peace." Caleb spread his arms to display his pleasure with the forest.

"Hmm, well we'll leave you to your peace."

During the cat and mouse exchange, Sarah did not utter a word. She gathered her stuff on Rayne's cue and the two left. They walked quickly. Rayne was comfortable with the path now. The coyote followed two-hundred yards behind them. Sarah was concerned they would be attacked but Rayne was very much the opposite. She was comforted by its presence. The crows overhead had also become a source of contentment.

At the car Sarah finally found her voice without stuttering, "Wow! That was scary weird."

"I guess. I don't know about scary weird but a little strange, yes."

"Do you think he was following us all along?"

"No. I really think that this is a place he goes to for peace."

"He freaks me out. At first I didn't realize that I had seen him before. He hangs out with that pack of kids, the ones that don't go to school but find themselves at our library a lot."

"Seriously Sarah? The library is a public place."

"But they're so creepy and they don't seem like the library type."

"I can't argue with that. There is something different about them and I'll admit, I am actually kinda curious."

"I don't think you should be too curious. Who knows what they are into? They don't even go to school. They're total dropouts. It's like they're gypsies or witches or something!"

"Sarah, don't start labeling them. You don't even know them."

"Sorry I'm calling it like I see it, they give me the he-bee-gee-bees. I'm keeping my distance from them, you should too Rayne."

"Uh-uh." Rayne was distracted by a thought of Caleb.

"Seriously Rayne, stay away from them."

"Gotcha. Don't worry."

The ride home was quiet. When they pulled in front of Sarah's house she offered one last plea of concern. "How would your parents feel about these kids?"

"Don't worry Sarah. I'll be fine. See you tomorrow." She stated frustratingly.

Rayne went into her house and it was quiet. Her parents were gone. They left a note stating they went shopping. If she wanted to meet them for dinner she could reach them on their cell. There were still a few hours of daylight and Rayne could not shake her curiosity. She got back in her car and drove to the forest.

The light that filtered through the trees shifted and the path appeared different during this time of day. She still made it to the spot she had been earlier where Caleb appeared. It was empty but like earlier, it did not feel empty. She had walked around the site twice until he stepped right behind her. She felt a breath on the back of her neck, causing her to spin around and jump back. She was alarmed with how she never heard his approach but he was able to get so close.

"You came back. Why?" Caleb kept his head down, not watching her as he spoke.

"Where did you come from? I didn't even hear you?" Rayne's voice was dry as she spoke.

"I was here all along. Why did you come back?" Now Caleb was hovering over her.

"I don't know. There is something about this place. I… I like it here. I think I've dreamt of it."

"You aren't afraid to be here alone? You aren't afraid of me?"

"Should I be?"

"Most people don't hike up here alone and I see how people look at me, how your friend looked at me. There is fear in their eyes. And to answer your question… no, you shouldn't be afraid of me, as a matter of fact I should be the one afraid of you."

"What do you mean by that?"

"Another time. Where is your friend? She seemed… odd."

"Sarah, she just worries a lot. I took her home." Rayne shrugged as she responded.

"So you are here alone? Does anyone know you are up here?" Caleb was a bit put-off as he questioned Rayne.

"You asked that earlier. Are you sure I shouldn't be worried?"

"I did ask earlier and for some reason you lied to me. You weren't meeting anyone up here. It's not safe to be out in a place like this alone. Bad things happen to nice people."

"So it's safe for you because you aren't a nice person? How do you know I'm nice?" Again, Rayne was being curt with him.

"I know enough… and I am nice enough. You should go. I'll walk you to your car. It's getting dark through the path."

"What if I'm not ready to go?"

"Well I've decided it is time for you to go. Come on."

Rayne was not happy that he had been so pushy with her but it was getting dark so she went with him. Their walk was quiet along the path but she felt as if he were communicating with her, not through words, but through a sensation or feeling. She did not understand it but a strange bond had already been created. It was what she had been trying to figure out with him since he had first caught her attention. He walked her to her car and still spoke no words. Without hesitation, she turned on the ignition and drove home.

Her dreams that night were as vivid as ever. She had seen an accident with another pedestrian killed, more dancing and chanting around a fire. This time in her dream Caleb was arm locked with a dark-haired girl. The girl was excited and seemed to be happy dancing with Caleb. This was the most disturbing part of Rayne's dream. Rayne was angry and a bit envious at the joy the girl was having while she danced with Caleb.

As her alarm went off, she woke in an unpleasant mood. It had not been lack of sleep that affected her morning, it was the dream. She was jealous of the girl in the dream.

Chapter 5

Church

Rayne had not been to church since her accident and earlier in the week she had told her parents she was finally ready to go with them. Unfortunately, the dream she had the night before her first day back to church had her in a bitter mood. The dream about the girl with Caleb was ruining her Sunday. Now she had to go greet people she had not seen in weeks while struggling with a bad attitude. She was quiet during breakfast and on the drive. Her parents did not hassle her about her less-than-friendly demeanor because they thought she might be feeling nervous.

Everyone seemed delighted to see Rayne. A few people in the congregation lined up to chat with her and exchange pleasantries. Socializing while pretending to be happy was not what she wanted to do. What she really wanted to do was sit in the back row and try to seek strength anonymously. Instead, she was front row being praised for her strengths in healing. Rayne did not feel strong, she felt distracted.

Her friends in the youth group were ecstatic to see her, especially Scott Gordon. He was a childhood friend and always showed an interest in Rayne. It was hard for him stay away from her when she was in the hospital but no one was allowed, only family members.

Scott Gordon was nice and funny. Rayne enjoyed her time with him now that he had matured. Sarah liked him too but he had no interest in her. Scott was fit and handsome. He was six foot one with an all American look. His eyes were hazel blue and his hair was dark blond. He was incredibly naïve but when he spoke, he had the attention of any girl. Rayne had always seen him as a friend and nothing more. They had been friends too long for any genuine intimacy. She had watched as he grew through his awkward stage. He was a nuisance as a child, always bothering Rayne. Now he was a mature handsome young man that was happy to see her safe and well.

When the service was over he stopped her on the way out. "Hey, glad you're okay. I would have visited but no one was allowed and at school you were always surrounded by a crowd."

"That's okay, I understand. I wasn't good company anyway. I slept a lot."

"You look good, I mean you look like you're recovering well. Do you want to go to dinner sometime this week?" Scott was doing what he could to spend some time with Rayne.

"I'll have to check with my parents. They are so stressed about me now I'm lucky if I can be out of their sight. Should I see if Sarah wants to come?"

"If it makes your parents feel better, sure."

"Okay, I'll call you."

Scott hugged her and said goodbye.

When Sarah noticed the two talking she waited for Scott to walk away before she approached Rayne. "It looks like Scott is happy to see you." Her tone seemed catty.

"I guess."

"What did he have to say?"

"The usual you know; glad you're okay, good to see you, do you want to go to dinner this week?"

"Seriously? He asked you to dinner?"

"Yeah, I told him I would ask my parents and I asked him if we should invite you."

"Really? What did he say?"

"He said it sounded like a good idea." Rayne knew Sarah liked Scott and she tried to be evasive so that she did not get her friend's hopes up.

"Yay! Let me ask my parents too." Sarah's excitement was obvious.

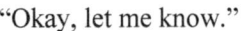

"Okay, let me know."

Rayne walked over to meet her parents as they managed to squeeze through the crowd of people. Rayne was quiet on the drive and during their lunch. Janie was concerned. "Is everything okay Rayne?"

"Yeah mom. Just distracted but I'm okay. Oh hey, Scott wants to go to dinner sometime this week. I told him I would have to ask you guys."

"You mean like a date?"

"I don't think so. Sarah is invited too. He didn't make it seem like he was asking me for a date. It's Scott… it's definitely not a date." Rayne rolled her eyes as she responded.

"I guess it will be okay. It's probably good for you to get out more anyway." Tom was looking at Rayne through his rearview mirror and gave her a wink.

"I agree with your dad, you need more than the two of us in your social circle." Her mom laughed.

"But you guys are my favorite social circle. Besides, I am making new friends."

"Oh. Who are these new friends?"

"Well so far it's just one friend and I can't even say friend yet. Just someone I've met. His name is Caleb."

Her dad's tone was short, "*His* name is Caleb? And when did you meet *Caleb*?"

"He works at the grocery store. Don't worry, we aren't besties or anything."

"Will we be meeting Caleb any time soon?" Tom was pressing Rayne.

"He isn't that kind of friend dad."

"Well if he does become that kind of friend, we'll have to meet him."

"I'm pretty sure you don't have to worry about it dad okay? Now can we change the subject?" Rayne knew what to say to get her parents to get off her back. Since she had never shown any significant interest in boys her parents did not need to give her any rules about dating. Now, the mention of one boy and they start to harass her. There was nothing to say about Caleb. The family finished up their meal with small talk about Rayne's week back at school and hiking with Sarah. Rayne made sure to leave out her encounter with Caleb. Their ride home was quiet and Rayne was content with it.

Chapter 6

Frequent Encounters

Monday's had become exhausting. It was senior year and the preparation for graduation was more than Rayne had expected. Essays, exams, and an evolving personal life had her rushing around in a frenzy. Her eighteenth birthday was six weeks away and with everything going on, she did not have time to get excited about it. She never put any real emphasis into her birthdays, but to her parents eighteen was something to celebrate.

"Good morning, Rayne."

"Morning mom. I'm just gonna steal a quick bite. I have to get to school early and I will be home late. I have a date with the library tonight."

"You have a date at the library?"

"No mom, with the library. I have a paper I have to finish."

"Oh. I'll leave a plate of dinner in the fridge for you." Janie danced around the topic of her daughter's birthday. "So your birthday is less than a few months away. I know these things aren't big for you but it's your eighteenth and your dad and I would like to do something special." Her parents thought this birthday was significant since the accident. After her disappearance, they did not know if they would see their daughter again so celebrating her birthday seemed exceptionally special this year.

"Mom, please don't. I just have too much going on."

"I know Rayne but you know how your dad and I feel about this."

"I understand but really, I'm super busy."

"Okay, we'll talk about it later. Be careful driving home from the library tonight." Janie knew that talking to Rayne about a birthday party was a moot point. Her daughter did not like to make a spectacle of herself.

After school, Sarah did not need to go to the library so Scott offered to drive her home. Rayne was distracted when she walked in. Immediately, her distraction was jarred when she could feel him. He had become a sensation to her; a feeling. She looked up and his eyes were already locked on her. She blushed and looked back down.

She set her stuff down on a round table in the study section. After she found the book she needed, she went back to her seat and put her nose right into her work. He walked up behind her and as usual she felt that warmth on the back of her neck causing her hair to stand. There was emotional electricity that seemed to pulse in her when he was around.

He pulled up a chair next to her. "Alone again? It isn't safe to go out alone, even to the library."

"Yes. Alone again. I am a big girl. Besides, it's still light outside."

"When you leave it'll be dark. I'll walk you out."

"I think I can manage. I am sure your girlfriend won't be happy with you walking me out anyway." Rayne nodded her head toward the dark haired girl sitting on the chair in the reading section. She was the same girl from Rayne's dream. She was glaring in their direction.

"She's not my girlfriend. We are kind of family."

"Kind of?"

"Hard to explain. Maybe one day."

He was vague when he talked to Rayne about his personal life but he acted like he knew her forever. He came across as though he had a right to be genuinely concerned for her.

"Why don't you go to school here? Unless you've graduated already?"

"Home school. Our whole group is home schooled. A few of us graduate this year."

"So do I... graduate this year, not home school? Why home school?"

"We move around too much for traditional school. We've been here for about a year."

"Why do you move?"

"Work. We have to go where the work is."

"You mean work in a grocery store? Aren't there grocery stores everywhere?"

"No, that's just what I do for extra money. My family, the elders, are in construction."

"Elders?" Rayne had never heard of family members mentioned to as Elders.

"Yeah, we travel as a whole family and those that have been around the longest are referred to as elders."

"That's different. What's your nationality if you don't mind me asking?" Maybe it was a cultural thing she had thought.

"Me personally. I'm mostly Native American but my family is blended and diverse."

"I should've guessed. Well I kind of did but I didn't want to assume."

"Don't you have work to do? Finish before it gets too dark and remember, I am walking you out."

"Okay bossy. Will do." She was not sure if his sense of humor could handle her comment. He seemed so serious for someone his age. She assumed he was seventeen since they were both seniors.

Rayne finished what she could and gathered her stuff. She checked out the book she was using and instead of turning to get Caleb, she decided to head for the door alone. Just as she was reaching to open it, his hand was on the bar pushing it open. "I thought we had a deal. I was supposed to walk you out."

"I didn't want to bother you."

"I'll have you know, it bothers me that you didn't come get me so in not trying to bother me, you did bother me. When I said I wanted to walk you out, I meant it."

"Sorry. It's no big deal. I can walk myself to my car."

"This isn't an argument you're going to win."

"Fine, walk me out." The walk to the car was quiet. When she opened her door he finally spoke, "Rayne things aren't as safe as you think. I really wish you would be more careful."

"I am careful enough. Until a few weeks ago I'd never had a problem and I survived that little incident."

"You're lucky you survived. You could have been killed."

"How do you know about that?"

"I… read about it in the news."

"Hmm, well like I said, I survived. Don't worry, I am careful."

"Okay, I'll take your word. See you later."

"Bye." Rayne did not like that Caleb was on her case about being careful. He was worse than her parents. She did like that she got to see him. There was something about being around him that made her feel whole. She had never 'needed' to be around another person, not even her parents. The more she saw him the more she wanted to see him.

Chapter 7

Back to Helping the Homeless

It had been over a month since Rayne and Sarah made a delivery. Although the weather

was getting warmer, they had a stockpile of warm clothes and blankets for distribution

and Rayne was ready to get back out and help. Sarah was nervous about going, but she

knew it was important to Rayne. She also did not want her to go alone so she agreed to

help. Janie was worried too. Rayne was stubborn and would not take no for an answer

and her mom knew it. She reluctantly gave her blessing and the girls went about their

work.

At their first stop Sarah noticed the crows again. "Wow! There are so many up there.

Where do they all come from?"

"I don't know. I've noticed them lately too. It's like they are following us." Rayne

commented nonchalantly but almost joking, trying to get a chuckle out of Sarah.

The girls managed all of their deliveries and on their way back they noticed the group of

kids that Caleb hung around with. They were perched on a bus stop bench along the path

that Rayne and Sarah usually traveled. They collectively glared into Rayne's car and

Sarah shivered. "That gives me the creeps. I don't know what's worse, those kids or the crows."

"I'm sure they're harmless, both the kids and the birds." Rayne felt the need to defend them but she made sure not to seem defensive.

"I definitely disagree with you on that. They make my skin crawl. It just isn't normal behavior. I've seen old horror flicks that play out this way."

"Seriously Sarah, you have a way overactive imagination. Besides, horror flicks are fiction, you know 'fake, cannot happen in real life'."

"Well I don't know about 'cannot happen' because it appears to be happening. You don't think any of this is strange?"

"If the accident never happened, you probably wouldn't even notice any of it. I think you are being paranoid." Rayne did know it was peculiar behavior and it did just recently start happening but she did not see scary movie scenarios, especially in Caleb.

When Rayne got home after dropping Sarah off, her mom greeted her with a hug and the family sat for dinner. They talked about the day and her pending graduation. Janie tried to talk about having a birthday party for Rayne, but again she dodged the conversation. As they cleared the table, Janie asked Rayne to stop by the store on her way home tomorrow to pick up stuff for dinner.

"Sure I'll go for you. I'd be happy to. Matter of fact, it can be my new chore. I can do all the food shopping." Rayne volunteered eagerly.

"Wow, since when do you like shopping for food?"

"I figure I have to get used to it if I am ever gonna be on my own so why not start now?"

"Good plan and I get to benefit from it. I'll leave the list of what I need along with the money."

Rayne went to do her homework after talking with her mom, then some light reading and early to bed. She had thought she would get a long night's sleep until she was awoken in the middle of the night. She was not sure if she was dreaming but something jarred her awake. After a few minutes of laying silent in her bed she heard a pitchy sound then a few seconds later some whooping and coyote cries. It sounded like a large pack. Rayne had never heard them so close to her house before and she wondered why it had disturbed her sleep.

After putting her mind at ease, she managed to fall back to sleep. In the morning she made sure to get the money and list before she headed out the door. School passed slowly as Rayne watched the clock. She was distracted all day.

When the final bell rang, she could not wait to get to her car. Sarah met her there and Rayne realized she had forgotten about her. "Oh hey, I totally forgot, I have to go to the grocery store for my mom. Are you okay with that?"

"Let me ask my mom." Just as Sarah was dialing her mom, Scott walked up to his car. He was parked next to Rayne.

"Hey Rayne, Sarah what's up?" Scott walked toward Rayne.

"Not much. Ready to go home." Rayne was passive as she answered.

"Me too. Are we gonna do dinner sometime this week?"

"My mom hasn't said anything yet. I told her it would be you, Sarah and me." Rayne made sure to include all of their names to remind Scott that it would be the three of them.

"Dinner? What about dinner? Are we finally going to do this?" Sarah chimed in.

"Remember I mentioned Scott wanted to go out some night this week for dinner." Rayne could see Scott's face look puzzled.

"My mom isn't answering so I don't think I'll be going to the grocery store with you. I am totally in for dinner this week though. Let me know what night. Hey Scott, Rayne has to go to the grocery store, do you think you can drive me home?"

Sarah did not see the look of disappointment on Scott's face as he responded. "Sure, hop in. Let me know Rayne."

"Will do. See you guys." Rayne was happy to be going to the store alone. She did not want to defend Caleb to Sarah.

The parking lot was half empty but Rayne parked at the farthest spot. She looked around the lot before she entered the store but did not see what she was looking for. Inside the store she looked at the kids bagging the groceries, still she did not see what she was looking for. Giving up the search, Rayne started her shopping. She had nearly gotten to the last aisle when she felt him behind her. "Hey, this is becoming a habit." She liked his deep voice.

"Not a habit, you work here and I have to shop."

"I don't mean you being here. I mean running into you."

"It's not like I am trying to run into you. You just happen to be at all the places I need to go."

"Works for me." Caleb had a sweet smirk on his face. "Where else do you go so I can make sure to run into you everywhere?"

"Besides school, the library and here, I go to church or stay home. I'm a bore."

"Hmm well, I guess you won't have to worry about running into me at either of those places. You'll just have to go shopping or to the library more. Or I could sign up for school."

"That's pointless, the years almost over."

"It isn't pointless if I get to see you more."

"Why do you want to see me more? You don't even know me."

"And I'll never get to know you if I don't get a chance to see you more."

Rayne felt a heat she had never felt before and she could tell her cheeks were crimson. He was bossy and forward but she was growing to like it. "My guess is you'll find a way to run into me more." She was confident with her snappy response.

"I'll take that as an invite."

"Take it how you will. Now if I can finish my shopping…" Rayne tried her hardest not to smile as she walked away from him. She knew he was still looking at her, she could always feel his eyes.

She finished her shopping and pushed the cart to her car. All part of the new routine, he was at her car ready to take her cart. "Can I convince you to go out to eat sometime?" He was confident when he asked.

Rayne was temporarily at a loss for words. He stood stoic waiting for her answer which made her feel more intimidated. Finally, she managed to squeak out, "Sure, I like to eat."

He laughed at her response. "Well that's good, it's kind of necessary."

She blushed again, feeling like a fool for what she had said. She had become irritated that he laughed and she huffed as she got in her car. "Rayne, I didn't mean to laugh at you. It's just you make me laugh. I don't do that much." She did notice that until they had actually started talking, he did not smile much and he had never laughed.

"Fine, I made you laugh. Do I get an award now?"

"Don't be like that. Really, I like that you make me laugh. It's… refreshing." Caleb was sincere when he spoke. The way Rayne made him feel was new, strange, and happy. Feelings that were foreign to him.

"Okay, I'm over it. So should I get your number?"

"I don't have a phone. We don't carry them."

"Not even for an emergency?"

"No, we have no need for them. We have other means, even in an emergency."

"We? Who's we?"

"My family."

"Oh, okay. How will we set up a time? I have to get permission first then I'll have to let you know." Rayne was having difficulty maintaining her concern of Caleb's lack of communication.

"I will see you again, soon. You can tell me then. Now drive safe." Caleb walked away with the cart and she sat dumbfound for a minute. As she drove away she tried to imagine anyone not having a phone, especially a teenager. The concept was foreign to her.

After she unloaded the groceries into the house, her mom thanked her for helping. Rayne took the opportunity to ask her mom if she could go out to eat with a friend.

"Oh, that's right. Scott and Sarah wanted you to go with them."

"No mom, it's the new friend I mentioned before. Remember, his name is Caleb?"

"Caleb, that's right. I think I have heard his name once before. Is he new to the area?"

"Well kind of. He and his siblings are home-schooled and if I didn't mention it yet, I met him at the library."

"I guess we could talk to your dad and see what he thinks."

"Thank you mom." Rayne kissed Janie's cheek and went to her room to do her homework. Later that night at dinner Janie brought up the subject of the date and Tom looked apprehensive.

"He wants to take you to dinner? Do we get to meet him first?"

"Dad you worry too much. I will see if I can have him over to meet you. I was going to dinner this week with Scott and Sarah anyway so I'll just ask Caleb to go with us."

"Rayne, we haven't had to talk about this since you were in sixth grade because oddly, it's never come up. If you recall, no single dates before you're eighteen."

"I know dad. This isn't a real date, it's just getting something to eat with a friend but if it will make you happy I promise I'll ask Scott and Sarah."

"I know you don't think it's a date but what's his name..." Janie chimed in "Caleb". Tom finished, "Caleb might think otherwise. I am sure to him, this is a date."

"Dad seriously, trust me. I'll be fine and it's just dinner."

"Ask your other friends and if they are okay to go then you have my blessing."

Rayne was happy with that. She could work with Scott and Sarah. She had hoped Caleb could. "Thank you dad." She walked over and gave him a squeeze and kiss on the cheek.

Chapter 8

The Date

The girls left early for school. They pulled into the school parking lot and gathered their things. Just as they were getting out of the car Caleb walked up to Rayne's side of the car. "Hey, you're early today."

"Oh wow! Where did you come from? I didn't even see you when I pulled into the lot." Although Rayne was excited to see Caleb, she acted surprised so Sarah would stay off her case.

"I was sitting right over there." He gestured to where his friends were sitting. "So what's the answer? Dinner?"

"Umm well my parents said yes but…" Rayne stuttered her answer.

"But what?"

"Well, I have to bring other friends. I think Sarah and Scott would be perfect. I'm sure you'll like them and I think you and Sarah have already met." She looked over at Sarah and gave her a wink.

"I'll have to think about it. I don't even know if I like *you*. I guess it will have to do." He was saved by his subtly charming grin and struggling sense of humor.

Rayne looked chagrin, like she had just taken a blow to her self-esteem. "I guess I don't know how to take that. Are you sure you want to go with us?"

"Hey, I was just kidding. Of course I want you to go. Do you think I would've asked if I didn't want to go? Lighten up. We'll see how your friends work out."

"I think you're going to have to work on your sense of humor. Do you have a night picked out?" Rayne forced a humiliated smile as she spoke.

"How about Friday night?"

"Sounds good. I'll ask but I'm sure it'll be fine. Don't forget to brush up on your humor. Scott and Sarah might not take you as lightly as I do."

"You call that lightly? Just remember, I'm not trying to impress Scott and Sarah. It's you I like to see smile." Caleb was steady as he spoke.

Rayne was getting used to blushing at everything Caleb said. "Okay, Friday it is. 6:00 okay with you?"

"Meet me at the market at 6:00." Caleb walked back over to his friends as Rayne watched him leave.

As usual, Sarah did not say a word during the entire exchange. When Caleb was out of earshot she chastised Rayne for not asking her if it were okay to go to dinner with the stranger.

"Sarah, he isn't a stranger. I've been talking to him over the past few weeks I just haven't told anyone. You've been around him. He isn't a stranger to you. Besides, Scott and I were the ones who got this whole thing started. You were invited just like Caleb was."

"Just because I've been around him doesn't mean I know him. I told you he and his friends creep me out." Sarah hid her hurt feelings about Rayne making sure that she was positioned at the same status Caleb was.

"Well this will be an opportunity to change your mind. Now hopefully Scott will be up to going as a foursome."

"I didn't tell you I was up for going! Not with him at least. Rayne you really should have asked me."

"Come on Sarah, besides I know you kind of like Scott. If Caleb is with me, you and Scott will have to talk more."

"Fine! If Scott goes I'll go." Sarah huffed.

"Thank you Sarah. I'm sure it'll be fun."

At lunch the girls talked to Scott about going to dinner. Rayne let him know her parents said yes, she did not mention Caleb going.

"So how about Friday night? 6:00? Are you in?" Rayne had an upbeat tone in her voice when she asked him. Sarah looked a little disapproving because she knew Rayne was waiting to drop the 'Caleb' bomb on him.

"Sure, sounds good. Where are we going?" Scott really wanted to go alone with Rayne but if they had to include Sarah just so he could see her, he would.

"Not sure yet." Rayne did not know if she should make the decision as to where to eat or leave it up to Caleb.

"Okay. Where are we meeting?" Jacob was excited.

"S B Market on Grand."

"That's a strange place to meet up." Scott sounded puzzled as he looked to Rayne.

"Yeah but we have to pick someone else up." Rayne was smiling when she answered.

"Oh really, who? Someone I know?"

"Not sure. His name is Caleb. He doesn't go to school here but works at the market."

"Okay, sounds good." Scott was hopeful that Caleb was going to be Sarah's date and this all might work out for him.

The rest of the week had passed slowly for Rayne. She asked her mom if she needed her to go to the store for anything but the house was fully stocked. She stopped by the library to do some homework and see if Caleb was there. No Caleb. She kept her attention focused on homework and book reports. The end of the school year was getting close and there were a lot of tests that seniors had to take so Rayne used her time to study.

Friday had finally arrived and Rayne's stomach was in knots. For the first time ever, she was concerned about what she was going to wear when she walked out the door. She struggled applying make-up and made sure to spritz some perfume on her shirt and hair.

When she went to hug her parents' good-bye, they noticed her appearance. "Wow, look at you. So this must be a real date."

"No it isn't. I just felt like a change."

"Call it what you will. You look beautiful. Have fun and be home by 10:00." Her dad's tone was light as he chucked while he spoke but she knew he was serious.

"I will. Thank you. Love you."

"Love you back. Be careful."

When Rayne stopped to pick up Sarah she noticed that she had make-up on too. Both girls stepped up their game for the night. The girls chattered on their way to the market, mostly small talk. They were both nervous. Rayne pulled into the lot and drove over to Scott's truck. "Do you want to ride in my car? We will all fit and it would be easier." Scott agreed and went around, getting in behind Rayne. No one noticed Caleb suddenly appear. "Wow, you're seriously stealth." Rayne was stressed but quick with wit.

Sarah took the opportunity to use Caleb's height to get in the back seat with Scott. Caleb was tall, but so was Scott. When he sat in the seat, Rayne introduced them and the tension was thick. Both of the guys barely said hey to each other and it was as if an unspoken battle had already started between them. Rayne could sense it but Sarah was oblivious. She was in the back seat with Scott and nothing else mattered.

Rayne decided to break the short silence and heavy tension with a suggestion of where to eat. They all decided on Mexican food at La Unica in Old Town. The food was cheap and the ambiance was perfect.

In the restaurant the girls sat first and sensing that they both wanted to sit next to Rayne, Caleb slid in next to her quickly. Sarah smiled wide as Scott sat next to her. They ordered and the girls did the talking. Finally Scott decided to take on the challenge of starting a conversation with Caleb. "So I haven't seen you at school, where do you go?"

"Home school. We move too much for traditional schools." Caleb's eyes scanned the room while he responded. Scott was happy to hear that he moves a lot. Maybe he would be leaving Lakeland Village soon.

"Why do you move so much?" Scott had an unintentional smile as he inquired.

"We go where the work is. My family is in construction, seasonal work. Some states pay more but they only build during the warm months." Caleb decided to give him all the information he would be asking for so he would stop asking questions.

"Your whole family moves together? Like a caravan? Do you own homes or just live out of hotels?" Caleb could have done without Scott's inquisition.

"Yes, we all move together like a caravan. We have no need to own homes if we don't spend much time in one place right? So why would we waste money on a home?" He managed to partially answer his question without giving away too much information about his nomadic life.

Rayne jumped into the conversation "It must be exciting to move around and see so much. My family is kind of rooted here. You know, pillars in the community."

"We like it. We forgo any true obligations to being rooted anywhere. Pillars we are not." He smirked after he said that. This was part of what Rayne liked about him, mystery.

Of course Sarah needed to add her two cents hoping that it would catch Scott's attention. "So you are like a… gypsy? Hmm, I guess it makes sense now."

"No we are not like… gypsies. I would accept nomads but gypsies, no." His nostrils flared when he answered and Sarah knew to back down but did not want to cower.

"Okay, okay. You're not gypsies, your nomads. Sorry to offend." She giggled a little afterward to lighten the moment. Rayne was happy the food arrived. She was ready for a shift in conversations.

They ate quietly. Caleb held an odd position while he ate. It looked as if he were guarding his food. His hand curved around his plate like a dam. Rayne hoped Sarah would not mention it and to her relief she did not.

Scott, Rayne, and Sarah talked a little more when their plates were cleared. Caleb seemed tired. There was plenty of time before Rayne had to be back home but Caleb suggested they go back to drop him off. Rayne was disappointed. He did not seem like the Caleb she had talked to every other time. She did not argue and the four of them paid for their check and went to the car. The ride back was quiet and short.

When Rayne parked they all got out of the car. Caleb was the first to walk away. He shook Scott's and Sarah's hand and told Rayne thank you. This was not the ending she had imagined. Of course Scott was content with the exchange and he gave Sarah a quick hug and went over to give Rayne a lingering hug. Caleb watched from a distance, none of the three could see him. They parted and Rayne drove Sarah home.

Sarah was the first to start talking. "That was… strange."

"What do you mean by strange?"

"Caleb. Did you know all of that about him? And did you see the way he ate? So do you think Scott likes me? He looked so good tonight. I wish he would've kissed me." At that point Sarah was just rambling.

"Caleb isn't strange, he's just different. I did know about him, what's the big deal? He ate fine. Do you think people in Europe eat like us? We're all different. Seriously Sarah, you're so… dramatic sometimes." A minute of quiet passed before Sarah piped in again.

"Well, do you think Scott likes me or what?"

"I dunno Sarah. Why don't you ask Scott if he likes you?" With that they were in front of Sarah's house.

"Let me know if you want to do anything this weekend. I don't think my parents have anything going on." Sarah was hoping to have a get together with Scott again.

"I will. I think I might just go hiking again."

"Huh, hiking. What's the sudden interest in hiking?"

"I've just been feeling the need to clear my head. Plus it's good exercise." Rayne knew Sarah was no exercise enthusiast and their last hike together was interrupted by Caleb, her not-so-favorite person, so she probably would not want to go which is what she was hoping for.

"Okay, well if you decide to do anything other than hike, let me know." Rayne watched as Sarah got into her house then she drove to hers.

At home her parents were surprised she was home before her curfew. She reminded them that it was just dinner.

Normally it would have been too early to go to bed but Rayne planned to get up with the sun to go hiking. She went and read in her room. She was unable to focus on her book as she replayed dinner in her head. Caleb did not look as spirited as he usually was. At that moment she realized that she had not been dreaming as much over the past few nights. Strangely she missed the dreams, although they robbed her of a good night's sleep. She dozed off without realizing it.

A few hours into her sleep, the sound of coyotes woke her. They were crying and calling to each other as they chased their screeching prey. Then within ten minutes the sound of sirens roared on the main road outside of her housing area. Rayne was used to the all-too-common sound. There were always accidents on that road and often times, they were fatalities. She was grateful she had not become a fatality herself. After that thought, she fell back into a deep sleep.

Chapter 9

Caleb's Return

Saturday morning, Rayne realized she had a dream during the night after she woke from the coyotes and sirens. She tried to recall it and as images and sensations came back to her, she felt confused by them. The dream was chaotic and wild, almost like the coyotes that disturbed her sleep. There was running and a wild, nearly rabid feeling that consumed her. She felt like she had been taken out of her bed. Now that it was morning, she was tired but refreshed and more than ready for her hike. She nearly inhaled a huge breakfast and packed a backpack with water and trail food.

Her mom reminded her to keep her phone on and bring her pepper spray then asked which path she would be on in case they needed to send out a hunting party. She laughed as she said that but she still worried for her daughter. Rayne reminded her she was nearly old enough to vote which made her old enough to remember to be careful. Janie usually let Rayne act independently but she was getting bolder about what she was saying and doing. "You don't need to be smart about it, I just worry and I always will."

"I know mom. I'll be okay. I've been in this area a few times now and it is totally safe."

"Nothing is totally safe. I hope you recognize that."

"I get it mom. I'll be careful but don't freak out. Sometimes the cell signal doesn't work up there but my pepper spray will. I'll bring the zapper for extra precaution."

"Where is it you said you go?"

"It's the trails right past The Lookout and right before Hell's Kitchen."

"Rayne, I didn't realize you were hiking in that area. With all those bikers around, you think it's safe?"

"Yes mom I think it's safe. They're bikers not hikers. They have no interest in pulling off the road to climb a trail. I think the wild life up there is more of a threat."

"I think bikers are the wild life and by the way, you aren't winning your argument by making me worry about you walking around wolves or any other wild animals."

"It's the Cleveland National Forest mom, there are no wolves. Mountain lions yes but wolves, no." Rayne never told her mom that she was going alone. Janie assumed Sarah would be with her.

"Rayne, stop. Just be careful."

"Okay, I'll stop. Gonna go now. I'll text you when I go in and come out. Love you." She gave her mom an over the shoulder hug as Janie focused on the newspaper.

"Love you too." Janie patted Rayne's arm.

Rayne stopped at the store before she went up the hill. She walked through the store to see if Caleb was there. She had wondered if he was okay since things seemed awkward at dinner. He was nowhere to be found, she even checked the parking lot. She started her car and looked up to see a slew of crows perched on the phone wires. Their beaks and eyes were facing her direction. It was the first time she truly acknowledged the sense that it seemed as though they were almost communicating with her.

It was a strange idea that she quickly dismissed as she pulled out of the lot. She was up the hill and parked within fifteen minutes. She text her mom that the ranger station was five-hundred yards away and waited for a response before she got out of her car. After her mom told her to be safe she threw her backpack on and started along the path.

The local birds were out and chirping but the sounds started to subside as Rayne got farther along the path. She passed the fire pit that was situated in the middle of the first day-picnic campsite and headed through the thicker part of the path. The silence had become heavy.

Rayne could feel her pulse quicken as she noticed how intensely quiet her surroundings had become. Her pace slowed as she went deeper in. She tried to focus her ears on anything she might be missing. A few minutes passed and suddenly she heard a crackle as something dropped above her. She jumped when a pinecone plopped in front of her. There was nothing in the tree that would cause it to fall. She picked it up and looked around. After calming her nerves, she started moving forward again.

Another snap quietly echoed as she was about to round the trail. This time it sounded like it was on the ground and whatever it was that caused the stick to snap had to be larger than a squirrel. She slowed her breathing so she could hear better and as she did, a coyote leapt from around the bend. She jumped back and as she did she lost her footing. Before she could get up the coyote was at her feet. She froze in panic as she tried to figure out what to do. She started to slowly pull her pepper spray out of her pocket. When she was getting into position to jump to her feet there was a low whistle and the coyote moved back. Caleb had come around the corner and the coyote sat. "You like to put yourself in dangerous predicaments. Didn't I tell you it isn't safe to come up here alone?"

Rayne inhaled deeply before she yelled at Caleb. "So why is it safe for you? And I'm not alone now am I?"

"It's safe for me because I know the area and I have no predators that can harm me."

"I know the area." She said mockingly, "And I carry pepper spray and a zapper-thingy."

"Believe me, that won't protect you. Next time you come up here let me know. I'll make sure to be your guide." Caleb was visibly irritated.

"I tried to come by your work this morning to see if you were there. Besides, anytime I come up here you're already here."

"You came by my work, to see if I was there?" He smiled and Rayne thought she saw his cheeks turn red.

"Yeah, because you left so quickly last night I was worried. I was just coming to check on you."

"You wanted to check on me?" He laughed to himself as he was confused by her concern. "I was tired and needed to get recharged. Sorry to worry you."

"You look a lot better today. I thought you were sick."

Caleb avoided talking about the situation anymore and averted the conversation to showing her around. She welcomed his invitation and the two worked their way through the path matching each other's stride.

He had brought her to a narrow clearing that had a creek running through it. There was a tree that had fallen and become a makeshift bridge. They made their way half way across and sat to take a break. "How do you know the area so well?"

"My family stays here. Well not here, farther in, but we know all the trails."

"Oh, I didn't realize anyone lived out here."

"Yeah, we prefer it. It is quiet and we don't worry about anyone being intrusive."

Rayne heard a stick crack on the trail behind them and she looked back. It was the coyote. It had been following them. Caleb looked at it for a second and it laid down. "Is it yours?" Rayne asked cautiously.

"He isn't mine exactly. We share a space. He knows my family and we know his."

Rayne was not sure what he meant by 'share a space'. She had guessed he meant they share the space of living in the forest. It would make sense that if he fed the animal it would find kinship with him. "So you all feel safe living out here?"

"We are very safe here. We don't fear nature. We appreciate it. It gives us life and security. It's people that need to be feared. There are some with darkness deep within their souls, a subtle evil hidden to the naked eye. That should be feared."

"How do you know I'm not dark inside?" Rayne was curious about Caleb's idea and wanted to keep him talking. She enjoyed his voice and how he appeared mentally, to be beyond his years.

"You have no dark in you. You are safe around my people but others will take advantage of your kindness, your goodness."

"Hah, you get all that from one dinner?"

"No, there are things I know." He ended the conversation. She was instinctively intrigued with what he was saying but she had the feeling that he would say no more. She was curious about his quiet and cool demeanor, but it also frustrated her. He never tried to impress her with money, words or tricks. He was just… him.

They sat in silence for a while. It was a comfortable silence. The two were content sitting on the log, no words. When the sensation became intense for Rayne, she shifted in her seat. She had never been like this around anyone. Caleb felt it too but it only confused him. There were emotions going through him that he had never been privy to. He was puzzled about how to react so he broke the silence.

"So what are your plans after high school?"

"Local college. I want to get general education out of the way. My parents will be paying for my first few years if I stay local. What about you?"

"Stay at the store for a while then get into the family business. No plans for college."

"Why no college? I bet they have plenty of grants and scholarships for you."

"Well you don't really need a college education for bagging groceries or building houses. Since we try to live off the land our needs are different."

"So no one has ever wanted more? I mean no one in your family."

"Not really. We see what more has done to people over many years. Destruction, corruption and violence, not worth it." Caleb kept his head down as he professed to Rayne.

"I agree but sometimes people go to school to learn how to change things… for the better."

"We don't need school for that. We make a difference and we live contently. Our lives are not excessive, we are humble."

"Well I guess I can't argue with that." Rayne knew she was getting nowhere with him. His argument was valid.

Caleb told her it was time to go. The day would be getting dark. It was an hour hike to her car. She agreed to go because she did not want to worry her mom but she also did not want to leave Caleb.

At her car he kept his distance and told her to drive safe. She wanted to stay but the sun was low in the sky. She said good bye and texted her mom. She hesitated before she pulled away. On the way down the mountain, she noticed the coyote along the tree line and crows perched all over the trees. She felt peaceful with them around. The same peace she felt around Caleb.

Chapter 10

Missing Caleb

The weekend was gone and the following week would be busy at school. It was time to start prepping for state tests. Spring had nearly arrived and the days were changing from cold to warm. Rayne and Sarah were too busy to go out on any more donation runs and since the accident, Rayne had lost interest in helping.

Rayne was struggling to focus and concentrate on graduation preparations. She found herself constantly thinking of Caleb. She stopped in the store a few times but he was never at work. She went to the library to study, hopeful that he would be there, but he never appeared. During the week she struggled with her busy schedule so there was not enough time to go for a hike. She was anxious for the weekend to come so she could try to get out on the trail.

Sarah and Scott ate lunch with her the entire week. It was usual for Sarah but Scott recently started making it a habit. They talked about Caleb but Rayne always stopped them before they got too far into a discomfort zone. Sarah was usually the one who started the conversation. She wanted to keep reminding Scott that Rayne was into Caleb. Sarah had realized that Scott liked Rayne but was hoping she would be able to redirect his attention and affection to her. Sarah had a crush on Scott throughout their high school years. This was the first year Rayne developed an interest in a boy. She never had an interest in Scott, partially because she did not know how to interpret his subtle hints. She liked Caleb more than she wanted to but she was guessing he did not feel the same way. There had been opportunities for him to kiss her but he never took advantage of the moment. She had always seen Scott as a friend. They had known each other since grade school. To her, he was not dropping any clues either. He was just being normal Scott. Only now he was around a little more often. She thought it was because he was interested in Sarah. Sarah had been not so subtle about her feelings for him during their entire senior year.

One afternoon as they were walking to class, Scott tried to set up another dinner. Rayne's response was passive but positive enough for Scott to get his hopes up. "I'll have to ask my parents. I am sure they won't mind though."

"Great, let me know."

"Will do. Talk to ya later."

Scott was enthusiastic about Rayne agreeing to go especially because she did not mention Sarah or Caleb going. That evening Rayne asked her parents and they said yes, just as she figured. It would be the same arrangement as the last dinner only this time Caleb would not be going. Rayne tried to find him to ask if he would go but he was nowhere to be found.

Friday came and the three met up for dinner. Scott was a little deflated when he saw Sarah with Rayne. He climbed into her back seat behind Sarah and they all made their way to Stadium Pizza. The tables were round and the scene was not intimate. It was all a completely unassuming situation but Scott was ecstatic that Caleb was not there and he finally got to sit next to Rayne. Sarah was tickled as she sat next to Scott. Rayne was distracted by the fact that she could not find Caleb.

After they ate, Scott asked Rayne if she wanted to play a few video games. He noticed she appeared to be distant and unconnected with the group. "No thank you. I'll just kick back and watch the rest of the football game. You two go play. I'll be fine." Sarah stood up and Scott reluctantly followed.

Rayne snuck off to her car to get her phone. She left it in her glove box. She was not sure what she was getting it for. She knew he would not have called. He did not have a phone and he did not know her number. She had just gotten the phone and was about to shut the car door when her peripheral vision caught movement.

There was a hedge that had grown along the edge of the parking lot and there next to it stood the coyote. The menacing looking creature had its eyes focused on her. For a second she had become excited. Usually, whenever there was a coyote around, Caleb was close by. She scanned the parking lot four times hoping he would appear but nothing. The coyote stayed and stared. It watched as she went back into the building. She turned to look outside once she was inside the doors and the creature was gone.

Scott and Sarah were sitting down when she got to the table. "Where did you go?"

"I had to get my phone. You know how my mom likes me to keep it close by. Are you guys done?"

Scott was done playing video games with Sarah and asked Rayne if she was ready to go. "Yeah, are you ready to head out?"

"Sure if you are besides, I have to get back home. Tomorrow is gonna be an early day for me."

"Early, on Saturday?" Scott was trying to keep the conversation going.

"Yeah, hiking. It's become one of my better habits."

Scott took this opportunity to invite himself to spend more time with Rayne. "I wouldn't mind some exercise. Do you want company?"

Rayne hesitated to answer but before she could get anything out, Sarah chimed in, "I'd like to go too." Sarah never seemed interested in hiking. The one time Rayne got her on a trail was the only time she had ever been on a hike.

"Uh… sure. I guess if you two want to come. I stay out for a long time when I go. It will be a couple hours of walking at least."

Scott recognized Rayne's hesitation and that it would be the three of them hiking but he was not going to get detoured by Sarah tagging along. "Let's do it. It will be fun besides, I've had enough pizza to get me through a hike for a couple hours."

They all got into Rayne's car and headed back to drop off Scott. Scott and Sarah chatted about the hike on the drive. Sarah was excited when she asked Rayne what time they were leaving for the hike. "I'm looking forward to tomorrow. What time are we heading up?"

Rayne was not looking forward to those two coming and her one last chance to get them to change their mind was now, "So, I like to be out the door by six or sun up." She had hoped they would take the bait and cancel.

"Six a.m. too easy. Do we bring anything special or are we gonna be those crazy hikers that eat tree bark and berries?" Sarah laughed at Scott's corny attempt at sarcastic wit.

With a flat tone Rayne answered him, "We'll stop at the store on the way up."

"See you at six." Scott closed the door and waved as they drove off.

Sarah started right in on Rayne. "Why do you seem mad at Scott?"

"I'm not mad at him. I'm just distracted right now. No biggy. Obviously he didn't think I was mad at him or he wouldn't have invited himself for tomorrow."

"I hope you're in a better mood tomorrow."

"My mood is fine. Seriously, I'm just distracted. Besides I can be how I want to be. It's my hike that you two intruded on."

"Wow! Where did that come from?" Right then they pulled in front of Sarah's house.

"Just lay off me a bit please. I'll be fine tomorrow." Deep inside Rayne knew this was not her typical behavior but she was confused and frustrated and she could not control herself. Beside the fact that she had not seen Caleb, she felt like there was an odd chaos going on in her head. She tried to think positively. Having Sarah and Scott with her will keep her mom happy.

She let her parents know she was home and was leaving early with Scott and Sarah so she would be going to bed early. She wanted to avoid having a conversation with them. The last thing she wanted to do was to talk about her birthday or her dinner with her friends. She did not want to talk to anyone except Caleb.

She was full of pizza and tired. She had wondered why the coyote was there without Caleb. It left her feeling lost. She could not get to sleep fast enough. She wanted to rest and clear her mind. In sleep, she found more confusion. She dreamt of another ring of fire with decorated people surrounding it. There was arguing and conversation. It was not the jovial dancing that she was used to seeing. The crowd was huge and the whole group was trying to get their individual point across.

Rayne felt trapped in the dream. She had the sensation of cowering like a small animal. In her dream she was forced to be quiet. She wanted to run and scream but fear of disappointment kept here there. The clarity of her dream made her feel as if she were there with all the people. The sound of her alarm shook her out of the dream and she was relieved, although she remembered the whole thing as vividly as if she were there.

She was slow getting ready and Sarah text her at 6:00 asking her where she was. Rayne let her know she was on her way and asked Sarah to call Scott to let him know they would be late. She brushed her teeth, grabbed a breakfast bar and kissed her parents goodbye. Scott was sitting with Sarah on her porch when she pulled up.

They all went to S B Market. When they walked in Rayne knew Caleb was not there. She could sense it, like a feeling on her skin. They got in the car and made their way up the hill. When Rayne parked, she had the same feeling she did in the store. She knew Caleb would be no where around. At least she would not have to worry about her two friends running into him and learning about his living in the forest.

Rayne was lethargic during the hike. She was not in a hurry. Although she loved her times in the trees, she needed to see Caleb more than she needed a hike. Sarah and Scott were well ahead of her. They only got to the second picnic site when they had decided to sit for a break. The two asked Rayne if she was feeling okay, that she looked tired. "I'm fine, just didn't get much sleep."

They all ate and passed the time with idle chit chat then made their way a little farther into the woods. Rayne decided she was more exhausted than she had thought and wanted to head back. Sarah, not being much of an outdoors girl, agreed.

At the car Scott asked if they wanted to go get something to eat later. Rayne turned the offer down but Sarah was quick to say yes. Rayne dropped the two off and went home to sleep.

Chapter 11

The Family

It was noon by the time Rayne got home. Her parents were getting ready for an overnight trip to San Diego. Rayne would be home alone for the night. She did not mind, she planned on sleeping. She had not been able to recharge after her dream filled night. Her mom told her what she made for her to eat and kissed her goodbye.

Rayne's new appetite had her more hungry than usual so she went in and ate the food her mom made for her, then went to nap. She slept deep for a while before the dream started. This time she was back in the local woods and confused. The coyotes and crows were there too. Trying to understand the dream, she felt like she had been placed there and it was strangely familiar. All the eyes were on her but she could not move. She heard voices, but was unable to single one out. Suddenly, she was fatigued from her dream and all that she was in the center of disappeared.

Although it started out as a nap, she had slept through the night. In the morning she opened her eyes feeling fully charged. She woke before the sun came up and noticed her windows open and curtains blowing in the breeze. She had not kept them open like that in a long time and did not remember opening them but thought maybe the exhaustion caused her to forget. She went and grabbed a breakfast bar and water and started to get ready for a hike. She was feeling hyper from her excessive sleep and wanted to exert a bit of the energy on the hill.

Rayne texted her mom to let her know where she was going in case her parents came home before she returned. This time she packed whatever snacks were in the house. She did not want waste time stopping by the store because she had a sense that once again, Caleb would not be there.

The air was starting to get warmer, but the morning still had a chill. She had on jeans and a tee shirt but made sure to grab a sweatshirt off the coat hook. Having her backpack in hand, she hurried to her car and made way to the trail.

As she paid attention to the road, she failed to notice all of the crows that seemed to be following her. They had eyes on her the moment she walked out her door and stayed fixed on her as she drove up the hill. There were a few coyotes along the tree line but they did not stand out enough to draw attention. When she pulled up to the parking area, there were no other cars. She texted her mom one more time to tell her she arrived, then shut down her cell phone.

The air was cooler as she stood in the shade. She pulled on her sweatshirt and grabbed her backpack as soon as she was zipped up. The trail was familiar now and she was quick to head into the woods.

She moved swiftly and felt as if she could see more clearly in every direction. She still had not noticed the crows around her, she had become easily numb to their presence as well as the presence of the coyotes. Her pace was steady and she walked for an hour without noticing how much ground she covered. She was in deeper than she had gone before and although the surroundings were new, Rayne felt as if she had been there before.

Walking at the same steady pace, she suddenly felt a shift behind her. She took a deep breath and turned to see what was there. Nothing. But now the air was heavy. She looked intently along the tree line but saw nothing. She turned to advance forward and was startled when she saw Caleb two feet in front of her. They stared at each other for a moment. Caleb looked worried, as if he had something to say but could not.

Rayne broke the silence. "Hey stranger, where've you been?" Caleb was silent still. Rayne tried to shift the tension. "You look like you've see a ghost. Is everything okay?"

Caleb finally spoke, "You need to come with me." He turned to walk away gesturing her to follow.

Rayne chuckled nervously and tried to make light of the situation. She responded using a pretend robot voice, "Yes sir, I will come with you." She had to pick up her pace to keep up with Caleb's stride. His legs were long and muscular. She trotted to catch up and stay by his side. She spoke again. "So, what's up with all the secrecy and where have you been?" Caleb remained tight lipped. Rayne was out of nervous humor, "Are you mad at me? What's going on?"

"Just come with me. Don't show fear. You will be safe." Caleb sounded firm.

"Don't show fear! Are you kidding me, those words alone cause me to fear. I'm going back. Sorry to have bothered you." Rayne stopped in her tracks.

Caleb stopped a few feet ahead of her. "It's too late. You can't go back, at least not completely. You need to come with me. It's the only way to know." Although his voice was firm, his plea was sincere and his face was washed with desperation.

"What do you mean I can't go back? What is it you need to know? Caleb you tell me not to show fear and right now that's all I feel."

He took her hand and looked beyond the surface of her eyes. "Rayne please come with me, I will take care of you. There is nothing to fear."

They stood for a minute and curiosity took over the part of Rayne's brain that just minutes before was being controlled by fear. Caleb could tell she would go with him and he started back on his descent into the woods. Rayne stayed at his side. The heavy feeling Rayne had just before Caleb appeared was getting heavier. She looked up at Caleb and could feel his need to keep her safe. She thought she heard him say stay calm but his mouth did not move.

She looked down from his face to see they entered a campsite. This time the site was full of others like Caleb. Every eye was on Rayne and she now recognized the tension she had been feeling. It was their presence, their glare, their questions. Again she heard Caleb's voice "Don't fear." His mouth did not budge.

Rayne thought to herself how familiar the people were. Strangely she knew their presence and almost accepted it. Caleb could feel she had become at ease with his family and sensed her acceptance of his family. Caleb's voice came again, inside her head. "I am pleased you accept them. They accept you too." Along with Caleb's voice was a soft humming of many other people. There were coyotes gathered together and crows lined the tree branches. The two walked through every area of the camp without speaking. All eyes followed and the hum continued. Rayne found herself feeling peaceful.

They completed their foot tour and Caleb walked her back toward the path into the forest. She thought to herself how she wanted to stay. It was so pleasant and peaceful. Caleb's voice chimed in again. "You can't stay now, not yet." His voice was soft and she knew she was supposed to leave and not look back. She walked with Caleb and did not notice they had made their way to her car without a word.

He smiled when he looked down on her. She felt like she was in a trance but she knew she was wide awake. "Rayne you are strong. You did well. I feel they have underestimated you and now they are more intrigued than ever. It is important for you to stay away for now. I will get you when it's time." He brushed her cheek softly with his left forefinger. "I know I've underestimated you, everything about you." He smiled and took her keys to open her door.

"Don't forget to text your mom." His last words reeled Rayne back into reality. She was spinning with emotion but keeping her mom from worrying was a priority. No faster than she looked down to text and bring her head back up, Caleb was gone.

Chapter 12

Bad Teacher

Rayne was in no hurry for her parents to come home. She was unsteady and semi-comatose from her morning adventure. The meeting with Caleb and his people had her in a daze. The sound of their humming remained her head. She was trying to understand the reality of the scene but there was no sense to it. It was completely surreal and unexplainable.

Her parents piled into the house and when they dropped their bags and started talking to Rayne, she had snapped out of her trance. "Rayne, are you okay honey?" Her mom looked concerned seeing Rayne stare out to nowhere. "Yeah mom, just kinda hungry and tired. How was your trip?"

"Well, you know, it *was* San Diego. That place is always perfect. We had a great time. How were things here?"

"Took a hike and rested. Nothing interesting." Rayne knew that was far from the truth. She could not explain what had happened, especially to her parents. She did not know who she could tell. Inside, she knew this was supposed to be kept for her alone. Rayne was a private person so she was not chomping at the bit to share.

"That's good, if you rested that probably means you needed it." Janie started dinner as she shared small talk with Rayne. Her dad put their bags in their bedroom and put his stuff away. He noticed his window open. "Rayne did you open our bedroom window or did we forget to close it when we left?"

"I didn't open it."

"Hmm, I am going to have to pay more attention to what I'm doing. Guess it's my old brain." He chuckled as he came into the kitchen.

They sat for dinner and Rayne mowed through her food with ravenous pleasure. "My goodness Rayne, are you sure you ate while we were gone? You're eating like an animal." Her mom had a half smile, grateful that Rayne enjoyed her cooking, but concerned about her new eating habits.

"Sorry mom, I just missed your cooking. Frozen dinners do the trick but there's nothing like Janie's homemade." Rayne smiled and tried to slow down. The truth was, she did not know why she was so hungry and could not eat fast enough. She kept her plate guarded and her head down while she ate.

"You know summer is coming quickly, so is your birthday. Any idea of what you want to do?" Lately, Tom struggled to find a common bond with Rayne so this conversation was his attempt.

"I am looking forward to summer, but spring barely got here. You I don't care much for my birthday." Rayne gulped her water.

"But it's your big one. The big one-eight, the big eighteen. Plus it's so close to graduation." Janie had a glowing mom smile.

"That's just it mom. My focus is on graduating, getting ready for community college then off to the big league. The relevance of my birthday is miniscule."

"Well I happen to think it's very relevant! Your accident… you know Rayne we thought we'd lost you. The fact that you're here to celebrate your birthday is… well… a miracle."

"Mom it isn't a miracle. It's because the doctors were able to fix me. Everyone who helped to make sure I'd live just did their job. That's what I've got to focus on, college and getting a job." Rayne stood to take her plate to the sink.

"Well I won't settle with doing nothing. If anything we can do a dinner or something." Janie was not going to let this issue rest until she could plan something.

"Okay fine mom, dinner but that's it." Rayne rolled her eyes playfully to entertain her parents.

She cleared her plate and excused herself to her room. She sat by her window and watched as the crows lined the electrical wires and surrounding trees. The sun was going down and the horizon was a palate of colors; pink, orange, yellow and pale blue. Rayne noticed how pretty the black birds looked in contrast to the watercolor sky. She felt a sense of calm.

Feeling relaxed, she decided to go to bed early. Her sleep was peaceful and absent of dreams. She woke early for school but immediately noticed she felt fatigued. She dressed for the day and gathered her bags. In the kitchen, her parents were drinking their coffee and reading the paper. They all exchanged morning greetings and smiles. Rayne was nearly too sluggish to smile. She got a breakfast bar and milk. It was an effort for her to swallow it down. She was a stark contrast to her behavior from the day before. "Rayne are you okay this morning? You look tired and you aren't eating much." Janie noticed everything about Rayne, even if she was not in direct eye-shot.

"Yeah mom, I'm good. Just a little tired this morning. Maybe I got too much sleep this weekend."

Janie put the back of her hand on Rayne's cheek to see if she had a fever. She felt normal. "Well if you feel like you're coming down with something, you better not be stubborn. You go to the nurse if you get worse."

"I will mom. Don't worry. I'm sure I'm fine." Rayne threw her backpack over her shoulder, grabbed her keys and mustered the energy to walk to her car. When she sat in the driver's seat she was nearly out of breath.

She drove over to Sarah's house and when the passenger door opened and Sarah plopped down she glanced at Rayne. "Are you okay? You look like... Well you look like hell."

"Yes, I'm fine. My mom asked the same thing. I'm just a little tired. I think I got too much sleep last night."

"Too much sleep. That's a first." Sarah chatted all the way to school. Rayne just listened and drove. They pulled into the school parking lot and Rayne found a spot close enough to the school entrance so that she would not have to walk far. She did not feel sick but she did not feel well. "Oh man, look at all those birds." Sarah was looking up. Rayne looked up to see what she was talking about. There were more crows than usual hanging out in the trees and on the lines. "Creepy!" Sarah cringed.

They walked in slowly. Rayne's pace was much slower than normal. Sarah was not going to ask her again how she was feeling. She knew her friend would snap at her. The first bell rang and Rayne barely made it to class; economy, not her favorite. The teacher's style was unconventionally perverted and not appropriate for high school students. Rayne found it uncomfortable from time to time. In this lesson, he was teaching how marketing techniques affect sales. She did not like the way he made sure to note how the power of suggestion sells product. He explained it using lipstick. He displayed to the class, with a tube of Revlon Red, just what he meant. Most of the class laughed as he held the tube and twisted it back and forth many times so that the red peeked through the top then disappeared. He also told the students to note the shape of the lipstick then he grinned and raised an eyebrow. His entire concept had crossed over to sexual harassment, which appeared to be his intent. The robust man plopped onto his chair looking pleased with himself. Rayne was irritated.

She never cared much for the teacher but this was the first time she had become truly irritated with him. All morning she was lethargic but for the first time that day, she seemed to have a strange burst of energy. The amount of anger she held for him as he stood in front of the class was pounding. She could feel her heartbeat in her ears. Mr. Louderbach stood up in front of the class with a pleasing grin for the laughter he had just evoked. Her irritation was elevating. She was no longer thinking rationally.

As she was about to push herself up from her seat she heard a voice in her head. "Rayne, no! Rayne breathe! Breathe." The voice was Caleb's. She shook her head in confusion then she heard it again but this time more calming. "Rayne breathe. In… out… breathe." Then more voices chimed in sounding melodic "breathe, breathe." Rayne was soothed. She sat back in her seat and was relaxed. She remained relaxed until the class was over.

The rest of Monday was uneventful. Throughout the day, Rayne tried to figure out why she was so infuriated with Mr. Louderbach and how she had heard Caleb in her thoughts. It reminded her of the day she walked through the campsite of Caleb's people. She had the same sense of unity and connection.

At home, she sat at her window trying to focus on her homework but thoughts of Caleb kept creeping in. She missed him. A lot. She had spent time with him over the weekend but her immediate need to see him was as strong as her need to breathe.

Janie called her out for dinner and she did not hear her the first time. She was distracted by deep thought. Finally Janie opened her door and told her again, "Rayne honey, dinner is ready." "Oh sorry mom. I guess I was distracted."

Rayne sat with her parents and was leisure about eating. She was still unconsciously thinking of Caleb. "You're so distracted Rayne. Is everything okay?"

"Yeah mom I'm just thinking about college." Rayne was quick to make an excuse.

"I can't believe how quickly this year has passed. It's amazing how it started and everything that's happened and now you're preparing for college. I'm so pleased with you. Rayne, you really are the child that any parent would be happy to have. I know you think I say that because you're my daughter, but you really are amazing."

Rayne blushed a little and rolled her eyes. "Okay mom. Thank you but I am just a typical kid."

"I don't agree with you so we'll leave it at that." Janie smiled fondly at her daughter. The family finished dinner and Rayne helped with the dishes. Afterward she excused herself to her room.

The sun was dropping behind the hills. Her window faced the view perfectly. She could see black birds everywhere and there were more flying in. Rayne had gotten so used to them, she did not notice them flocking. She had given up trying to do homework and decided to take a walk.

The early evening air was warm on her skin. She walked out toward the main street, not paying attention to where she was going. Before she realized it, she had walked more than two miles from her house. It became dark out and the air cooled a little. She wanted to keep moving in the direction she was going but she had heard the voice again. "Rayne, turn back." She shook her head a bit thinking it would make the voice dissipate then looked around her to see where it was coming from. There was nothing around her, only cars passing by and a lot of birds overhead, crows especially.

She took a few more steps forward and it came again. "Rayne, turn back." It was Caleb's voice and a crow flew right past her. She looked for him again. As she looked around it came again "Rayne, go home." This time she felt the wisp from the crow's wings and a dire need to go home. She turned and headed back. When she walked in the door her parents chastised her for being gone so long and not letting them know that she had even left or where she was going.

"I just needed to clear my mind. I'm sorry. I won't do it again." Understandingly, she had to readjust, her parents gave her a hug and went back into the living room to their nightly routine of watching the news. KCAL9 was just reporting about an attempted child abduction in Lakeland Village. The attempt occurred on the same street Rayne had just walked on. Her parents called her in to ask her if she noticed anything. They rewound the newscast so she could see it from the beginning.

"No I didn't see anything. Everything seemed fine while I was out there." Honestly Rayne did not remember much about the walk. She was distracted, which is why she did not notice how far she had walked. She did recall hearing Caleb's voice and knew it was in her head. He or *something* seemed to be warning her, but about what she did not know.

"I guess you can see why we worry. You never know what could happen. Well, we know what could happen and we don't want it to happen again." Janie gave Rayne a concerned mom look after she said that. Rayne flashed back to her accident. She still did not remember how she got injured or taken to the hospital. She only remembered that it felt like she had been hit by a truck.

"I'll be fine mom. Don't worry, I watch out for myself." She gave a fake smile and went back to her room. As she walked away she yelled back "I'm kinda tired. Gonna go to bed early tonight." She was tired.

Her head was barely on her pillow when she dozed off. She fell quickly into a deep sleep. The beginning part of her slumber was non-eventful. A few hours past her first deep breath of sleep, she was pulled into a dream. She was among a chattering group of people that sat around a campfire. It was a familiar setting, she had been there before and in her dream state she tried to remember if her previous visit was during wake hours or in her slumber. Things had become blurred for Rayne.

As she tried to understand what was being chattered about, Rayne struggled to hold herself in place. She was unsure if she was standing or sitting. She almost felt elevated, as if she were flying or floating. The sense she received from the chatter was of concern. Rayne heard her name a few times and being referenced to as "that girl". She also heard Caleb's voice. It appeared he was reasoning with the others. His demeanor was reassuring and demanding. He seemed to hold the floor more than anyone else in the crowd. He stood and sounded like a lawyer that was making a case.

There was a sudden shift about the group when someone spoke up and said something inaudible. Then, everyone looked in Rayne's direction. Suddenly she felt out of place. She had thought in her subconscious, that it was the same awkward feeling she had when she dreamt of going to school in her bra and underwear. Everyone was staring at her, she felt exposed. There was a panic that came over the group and also through Rayne. Suddenly she plunged into a sensation that she was falling through a bottomless black hole and in a matter of seconds she bolted awake. Her heart was pounding and she was panting as if out of breath.

As she tried to bring her heart rate back down she reflected on her dream. It felt so real being among the crowd. She sat up in her bed for a few minutes when fatigue took over and she laid back down and finished her night's sleep.

Chapter 13

Risky Walking

School was usually easy for Rayne, but the last few weeks she had slowed down with her studies and she was often tired in class. The most recent math test she had taken received a low grade. This was uncommon for Rayne but missing three assignments before the near failing grade was what had concerned her teacher.

Ms. Jenkins pulled Rayne aside after class and asked her if everything was okay. Rayne replied passively, "I'm fine. I've just got a lot on my mind lately. It's a little harder being a senior than I thought."

Ms. Jenkins understood, especially after her accident. Rayne had done well for a child that had gone through her ordeal. "If you need tutoring I can help you. If you need extra time I can give you that too but if it's something more than that I really recommend you see your counselor."

"I know Ms. Jenkins. Thank you. I will try to fix it myself. If I can't I'll go to Mr. Murray, I promise." Rayne wanted to leave Ms. Jenkins with some confidence that she would rectify her academic problem.

Rayne went to the library after school to focus on school work. She made sure to send her parents a text to let them know. They were becoming significantly more paranoid and she did not want to alarm them especially after her poor grade.

They responded letting her know they were okay with the library. She did all she could trying to catch up. Being away from her house did help with her distraction. After she finished the last missing assignment she gathered her things and left. Outside the door were Caleb and a couple kids from the campsite. Rayne's eyes grew, she did not expect them. She had been so engrossed in her math work she did not even sense them there.

"Rayne, you'll have to come back soon." Caleb looked weak when he spoke.

"Come back? Where? What's going on?" Rayne was exhausted and confused nearing the point of complete frustration. Over the past few weeks she was failing in school. She had seen and heard things she could not understand. She had become ravenously hungry but did not know what it was she was craving in order to fill the hunger.

"You'll have to come by Friday. Rayne it's important. I don't know how you're gonna do it but you need to come to camp after school." The group watched quietly as Caleb spoke. He turned to walk away before Rayne could respond.

The week passed slowly and Rayne grew weaker daily. She tried to figure out how she could get away Friday. She thought of Sarah's house for a sleep over but it was too close to home. Rayne did not hang out with any other girls.

Friday finally came and Rayne was out of time and ideas. In a last ditch effort, she had come up with a plan to tell her parents she was going to bed early then slip out her window. It was on the second floor but the part of the roof that protruded under her window sloped down toward the yard. Her drop would only be nine feet. She made sure to wear the right clothing for the evening and made her bed look like she was sleeping in it.

After she crawled through her window she closed it enough to look like it was completely closed then she put her screen back on. She shimmied down the tiles on the roof and hung over the ledge making sure not to tap on the rain gutter. The sun had been down for a few hours so it was easy to stay camouflaged in the dark. Rayne could not drive her car so she started the walk toward Caleb's camp.

The long dark street was one of the many unsafe streets to be a pedestrian on. It was poorly lit and in many spots, there were no sidewalks. There were paths worn in the dirt by the people that had walked the same route Rayne was walking. The traffic was steady on the two lane street.

After a few miles Rayne's legs were getting heavy. She was near one of the areas that she used to deliver coats and blankets. An uneasy feeling came over her. She usually gave people and situations the benefit of the doubt but since the accident, things had started to change. Rayne had changed. She could hear voices. She recognized the voices. They came from the same people she donated warm clothes and water to. Her steps grew shorter and the voices came nearer.

She was unable to make out the words but she sensed that whoever it was had come right upon her. Suddenly feeling lightheaded, a burst shot past the front her, then she heard the squealing of tires and brakes. Before her head hit the dirt ground, she looked toward the street and saw Caleb running at her and away from the cars that had just hit something. Everything went dark…

Chapter 14

Still No Answers

A rush of air flooded her lungs. Rayne woke up coughing. Her head was throbbing and she still had on the clothes she was wearing when she snuck out. The sun had not come up yet but she could tell she was in her room. Her window was open and the screen was on. She looked at her clock and the time said 5:34am. More than eight hours had passed and she did not remember getting to her bed.

She felt her head where the pounding was coming from. There was a lump on the side. She turned her light on and looked in the mirror. She was dirty and her hair was a mess. She looked like the homeless people she so often helped. "Homeless..." She started recalling the night. The voices as she walked and the screeching cars, the burst of what ever had rushed in front of her, seeing Caleb it was all coming back to her. She would not have believed it had happened if it were not for her tattered hair and dirty face. The lump on her head was also a painful reminder.

Her bed was dirty from her clothes. She did not know how she got into her bed. It was almost time for her parents to wake up and she needed to get cleaned up before they saw her. She had more energy than she had in a week. With a quick swoop she pulled off her dirty clothes and threw on her robe. She brought hiking clothes to put on after her shower.

Her parents were in the kitchen when she went in for breakfast. They exchanged morning greetings and Rayne pulled out some aspirin. Her head was still throbbing and now her stomach was keeping tune with its growling. As she devoured a breakfast the size of a lumberjack's meal, she talked of the hike she planned out.

"I'm glad to see you have your appetite back. Are you sure you're not going through growth spurts. You haven't had an eating pattern like this since you were a little girl. Sleep, eat, sleep, and eat. That's all you did for your fourth grade year." Janie had given up worrying about Rayne's new habits. She decided to chalk it up to high school and senioritis.

During breakfast her dad talked about another accident on Grand Ave. It was the road she was walking along last night. He complained how there were always accidents there because of the poor lighting and careless drivers. They believe the man may have been drunk and stumbled onto the road in front of a car.

She had been on Grand Avenue and remembered hearing cars skidding on the road but not much else. Rayne finished her food, kissed her parents goodbye, and told them she would be gone a few hours. They reminded her to text so they knew she was safe. She grabbed her sweat jacket, water and snack bag then bolted out the door. This time, she would drive her car.

Parking was open. There were not a lot of hikers. She kicked up dust when she pulled up to her usual parking spot. The air was warm and dry as she started on the path. Her comfort had become instant as she winded through the trees. The sounds that used to alarm her had become peaceful, nearly mute. With quickening steps, she neared the campsite. She walked forty-five minutes and had not reached Caleb yet. Suddenly, it dawned on her that they had moved. She walked farther in but not a sign of any of them. Looking up she noticed there were no birds. At that point, there were only sounds of occasional falling leaves.

Rayne sat on a log that a week ago, was the seat for many people in Caleb's camp. Just yesterday Caleb told her she needed to come back. She was confused and hungry. She munched on two of the granola bars she had and drank one of the bottles of water. Still there was not a single stir among the woods. Rayne waited an hour before she headed back.

At her car, she sat in her driver's seat and texted her mom. She waited again to see if he would appear. She waited in vain. He never came. She had hoped she could at least hear his voice, but nothing. Rayne texted her mom to tell her she was going to the library for a bit. That was the last place she had seen him and maybe he would go back there.

Without her school books, she did not have anything to study or read so she opted for the newspaper. The third page in on the local news was the accident that happened during the time she had been walking the night before. There was also a write up on the attempted child abduction. They emphasized to be on the lookout for further attempts. They gave a description of the car and young man. Rayne did not pay much attention to the article because she could not pull her thoughts from Caleb and for some reason the accidental death was nagging at her.

The guy that had been hit was a vagrant. He was a local to the area and had a prison record. He served a long prison sentence for aggravated rape. He had not reported his location to authorities although he was required to check in with his probation officer monthly. Rayne recognized his picture. She had given him a coat and blankets before. He seemed nice enough from what she could remember, never bothering her and always smiled.

The rest of the paper did not hold any interest for her. Rayne got her purse and keys and went to her car. The sun had warmed the asphalt and she pulled off her sweatshirt. She had noticed some caws from the crows on the electrical wires. They were back and she knew they were there for her.

The road was heavy with Saturday traffic. There were bikers and pedestrians everywhere. It was a nice day and Lakeland Village usually saw an influx of people on good weather days. There was any number of things to do within ten miles of Rayne's house. Lake

Elsinore was barely a mile away and was often full of boaters. There were skydivers jumping every twenty minutes and cyclists pedaling their way along the busy road. On sunny days bikers made up the larger population of road traffic. It was a favored place to ride along the Ortega Highway over to Pacific Coast Highway. The Ortega is where Rayne usually hiked. It's where Caleb's family lived.

She walked in the door and her parents were surprised to see her so soon. They asked how her day was and if she would be home for dinner. They planned to go out to eat but they would take her if she wanted to go. She told them she was fine with what was in the house and wanted to stay home.

The next few hours she caught up with her remaining school work and took a short nap. When she slept she remembered a little more from her night. The flash that blew past her was Caleb. During her dream everything slowed down and she remember seeing his face right before she blacked out, but he was hovering over something or someone.

Before she could dream any longer her parents came in to tell her goodbye. They planned on going to a movie after dinner and they wanted to make sure she did not want to join them. Rayne reassured them she wanted to stay home and she would be fine.

She stayed in her room and turned on her television. As she flipped through the channels, she noticed crows flocking outside. They started coming in droves. At her window she could see them everywhere then she looked down to her lawn to see Caleb. He was looking up at her. There was a static feeling in the air. She walked down to go out to meet him, but as she opened her door he was nearly in her face.

"Do you want to come in?" She was trying to understand what she was feeling as she spoke. He walked in and closed the door. He still had not said a word. He looked a bit like a zombie but with healthy skin. He looked around her house then he set his gaze on her. The quiet became unnerving for Rayne. "Caleb, are you planning on saying anything?" Still he did not talk. Her ears began to pound and her heart fluttered. She felt dizzy and needed to sit down. He kept his eyes on her.

"Rayne, why were you walking last night?" His voice was even.

"You said I needed to come back. I had to sneak out and couldn't drive my car. How else was I supposed to get to your camp?"

"I can't believe you tried to walk that road alone at night! Rayne you were almost attacked! I never would have told you to come if I knew you were going to do something stupid! So stupid Rayne!" She never heard him talk this aggressively. His nostrils were flared and his face red. He was angry.

"There was nothing around to attack me. I was perfectly fine. Was that you I saw? I knew it, I thought I imagined you were there but it was you. What happened?" Rayne still felt lightheaded and stayed seated.

"What do you remember?"

"Obviously not much if I had to get yelled at to remember you being there. I was walking then something kind of flashed by me. I'm guessing that was you but at the same time I felt dizzy like I did just now, so I started to fall. Before I was all the way down, I heard car tires skidding on the pavement and saw your face. Then I was out and woke up in my bed choking on my breath with a lump on my head."

"You don't know how you got here? I mean you don't remember?" Caleb seemed to be calming down.

"No I don't at all. I was dirty though and my hair was messed up. I was still in my clothes. You said I was going to be attacked. How do you know and by who?"

"Don't worry I took care of it. How is your head and how are you feeling?" Caleb was back to his calm self now.

"I still have a lump but I feel good. As a matter of fact, I felt good enough to hike to your camp today. I got all the way up there and no one was around? It's like you all never even existed there? I thought I was supposed to go back there. Caleb I am really confused with what's going on? How did you take care of it? Who was going to attack me?"

"We had to move, I'll take you another time. You have some time now so there is no rush to go back. You don't know the person who was coming for you but it won't happen again." He walked to her and brushed her cheek with his finger. She felt that electricity again, like static. He excited her more than ever. She did not want to move from the chair. He squatted down next to her and brushed her chin with his thumb. "Rayne, you'll have to watch your anger and you're going to have to be more careful on the streets. Listen to the voice. It will always guide you right."

He brushed his nose softly across her cheek and she could not move. He walked toward the door and as he reached for the handle he reminded her to be careful. He was gone before she could move a muscle. The door clicked and she tried to speak.

"What do you know about the voice? Anger, I never get angry." He was gone and did not hear a word she said but she had to get it out. She had wondered how he knew about the voice. It frustrated her that she had so many questions but never had enough time with Caleb to get them answered. Every time she was with him something new would happen and give her cause for more questions.

Chapter 15

Do What Caleb Says

Rayne stayed in for the remainder of the weekend. She did not know where his family's

new camp was and as much as she wanted to, she knew she could not go scout hundreds

of square miles to find him. Sunday her parents asked her to go with them to church. She

had not been in a while. She was feeling good so she decided it would be nice. She did

like the tradition she and her parents had on Sunday. Morning worship and afternoon

lunch was how she used to spend the last day of the weekend.

She was up early and put on her faded jeans and polo cardigan combo. She had always

dressed causal for church. The ride was short and they parked in the dirt lot. Most people

had already arrived to hear the music. Rayne was feeling good as she heard the last of the

morning's lyrical spirits.

They went to their seats in the balcony section. Rayne was listening to the pastor as she

started to notice all the people. She blinked her eyes a few times thinking that something

was wrong with her vision. There were different colors around all the patrons, almost like

a glow. They were faint colors and most had a soft hue to them but there were more than

a handful that had blurred faces with vivid almost wicked red and black colors around them. They stood out immensely and Rayne's ears started to burn when she looked at them. She struggled to sit through the rest of the service and did not hear a word spoken once the colors caught her attention. She looked at her parents to see if they might be experiencing the same thing. She did not want to interrupt the service so she decided to wait to ask them.

When the service was over everyone malingered out of the building. Rayne's parents had a tendency to stay and chat with others. They noticed Rayne seemed distant and asked if she was okay. She had a hard time responding because she felt that anger, the same anger she had in her class with Mr. Louderbach. She had given them the excuse she was hungry so they agreed to leave and get her to lunch. The car was comfortable and helped to make her immediately feel better.

Janie looked back and noticed Rayne seemed peaceful. "You look better sweetie. Maybe it was a little too warm out there for you."

"Not sure mom but I do know that I'm hungry." She smiled at her mom. She was just happy she was out of the building and away from the colors. There was no way to explain what she was feeling. She only had that problem once before and she still did not understand it. It was puzzling to be that annoyed for no reason at all. She decided not to ask her parents if they witnessed the glowing crowd.

Lunch was quiet, mostly small talk. Rayne was busy filling herself with tacos. She loved Don Jose's street tacos and did not bring her head up from her plate much. It was then that her parents settled on Don Jose's for her birthday dinner. They decided to quit bugging her to have a big bash and gave into a quaint dinner with friends. The three were pleased and Rayne swallowed down two more tacos.

Monday morning Rayne was up and ready for school. She let her parents know she would be late coming home because she had some work to catch up on at the library with Sarah and Scott so the three would probably go get a burger together when they were done.

Monday was normal as far as school went. The library was a different story. The three met up and walked around the fence to the library entrance. It was quiet inside and there were many open seats. They all gathered around a short table and soft chairs and pulled out their work. Fully focused on their own material, none of the group noticed a crowd of other teens come in.

The kids gathered in the corner. It was Caleb and he was with the dark haired gang she remembered from a past visit to the library. Rayne also recalled some of their faces from her day in Caleb's camp. She now felt the urgency of the pack. Her concentration was redirected to where they were standing. Scott and Sarah were still entranced in their work but Rayne was lost. She stood and walked in their direction. Caleb did not move his mouth but she knew his thoughts. "You need to come with us."

"Why? Where? I can't just leave my friends here. My mom thinks I'm with them."

"Call your mom and tell her you'll be a little later than you thought. Tell your friends you're going home."

"But I drive Sarah home. My mom is going to want to know why."

"Just tell her you're going to eat. Your friends don't need to know anything. Scott can drive Sarah home. I'm sure she won't mind."

"You expect me to go with you no questions asked?" Rayne did not realize the whole conversation was playing out in their thoughts.

"Yes."

Rayne did what she was told and feared to ask questions after that. Just as Caleb said, Sarah was more than happy to go home with Scott. Caleb got in the car with Rayne and told her to drive to his camp. As they drove Rayne noticed she felt fatigue. She parked and they trekked through the forest. She could hear stirring behind them and as they got closer to the new campsite, she realized the noise was from the rest of the kids who were in the library. They all entered the camp together and there was a large group gathered around a campfire.

As Caleb and Rayne approached they all hushed and stared at her. She heard a soft hum in her head and now realized it was coming from the family. Caleb led her to a seat by the fire and sat her down. She felt weak and relaxed. The flames from the fire danced and as she gazed upon it she started to fall into a trance. The humming in her head grew into chatter and suddenly she went limp.

While she slept by the fireside, she immersed into the sensation of floating like the fire. The tranquil feeling of peace and unity surrounded her when suddenly erratic chaos stirred her. She tried to wake from her deep state of sleep but she could not. There were many times in her life when she had bad dreams and managed to pull herself awake but this time she could not.

A split second after the chaos passed she heard tires skid. After the squeal of the tires, Caleb was shaking her to wake up. When she opened her eyes he was hovering over her face. "Are you okay?"

"Yeah. What happened? I fell asleep, how embarrassing." Rayne pulled her jacket snug over her shoulders.

"Don't be embarrassed, you were supposed to sleep." Caleb was the only one left at the campfire with her.

"Where did everyone go?" Rayne looked left and right.

"They left us to talk. Rayne have you noticed any changes lately?"

Rayne did not want to say anything because she thought she might sound crazy. "Well besides falling asleep at your camp, I don't think I've noticed changes. What changes are you talking about?"

"Rayne, I've heard you. We've all heard you. You have to tell me. What is different?"

Rayne did not want to say anything to Caleb. She made the excuse that she needed to get home because her mom would worry. She looked at her phone and noticed two hours had passed while she was there. It was dark and she panicked. "My mom is going to be worried. I told her I'd be home an hour ago." Rayne stood up but was dizzy and had to steady herself.

"Rayne you really should wait a minute. At least until you get your strength." His face looked pleading.

She had wondered how he knew she was weak. "I'll be fine. I just need to go home and get something to eat." She got back up to leave, but this time she was able to stay up.

"We need to talk. I'll walk you to your car." He took her by her arm and led her though the path. They walked in silence and he finally spoke when they got to her car. "Let me drive. You need to take it easy for the night."

"How will you get home?"

"I can walk. I don't mind. I just need to make sure you get home okay."

"It's too far to walk."

"Don't worry about it. Honestly I don't mind."

She gave in and let him drive while she texted her mom to let her know she was on her way. Her mom had sent two texts and tried to call once before Rayne had a chance to respond. "She's upset. I don't think she is going to let me out of the house after tonight."

"Rayne it was important that you came tonight. I know even if you won't admit it, you feel different. I know your anger. We all do, my people... my family."

"What do you mean? They don't know anything about me. I've never said a word to them and they've never spoken to me."

"Rayne I know you sense us. I know you hear us when we're not with you. You don't have to worry you can tell me."

"I really don't know what you're talking about." She stared down at her phone as she spoke.

"Soon enough you'll let me in. You won't be able to stay away and you'll finally talk."

He pulled up to her driveway as he said that. He turned off her car and she took her keys

from him.

"Thank you for driving. Enjoy your walk." She had the last word. Before he could say

anything else she turned and walked into her house.

Chapter 16

Birthday Aura's

It had been a week since Rayne last saw Caleb. Every day she waited to see if he would appear. She went to the library after school hoping for a glimpse of him but was disappointed every time.

Janie made plans for Rayne's birthday later that week and asked who all she wanted to invite. Rayne wanted Caleb but knew he would be the one guest that would not show. She gave her mom the short list of friends she asked for. Janie asked if her new friend would be coming. Rayne did not realize her mom was paying attention enough to mention Caleb. "No he won't be there mom. I haven't seen him lately."

"That's too bad. Your father and I were looking forward to meeting him." Janie gave her a smile to let her know she was sincere about wanting to meet Caleb. Rayne had never shown any interest in the boys she had known. Janie was grateful that she did not have to deal with a boy crazy daughter, but she did want Rayne to find someone she liked.

"No biggy. He'd probably feel out of place anyway. He's kind of different." Rayne was acting dismissive as she spoke.

"What do you mean different?"

"Well he's real quiet. His life is very different from ours." Rayne did not know what words to use when she described him. She did not want her mom to think he was a freak.

"Should I be worried? What kind of different?" Janie was paying full attention to Rayne's demeanor.

"No mom, there's nothing to worry about. He's just unique. His family lives as a group. They stay pretty tight-knit. They are the kind of people that do not use electronic devices, not even phones or televisions." Rayne hoped she was convincing her mom that Caleb was safe when Rayne herself did not know if he was truly safe. The one thing she knew for sure, he was mysterious and Janie did not need to know that.

"Well maybe one day we'll meet him. Either way I'm sure your birthday dinner will be great." Janie kissed Rayne on her forehead and left her alone.

Talking about Caleb to her mom made Rayne miss him more. She was not hearing the voices anymore and had not been weak since the night around the campfire. There were no more dreams or anything that could link her to Caleb. Rayne's constant thought had become Caleb.

Her birthday finally arrived and throughout the school day she wished she could contact Caleb. After school she and Sarah drove home. Sarah raved about getting together for Rayne's birthday. Rayne knew that Sarah was more excited about Scott going. There would be two other friends, but Sarah was only interested in Scott. The night had not started, but Rayne was ready to be done with it.

Rayne drove to the restaurant with her parents while her friends drove together. Inside there was a section blocked off for her party. There were more chairs than Rayne had expected but she ignored it. They all sat after they gave Rayne her birthday hugs.

While everyone talked, the time passed slowly. There was a sudden hush over the group. Rayne looked up as Caleb walked toward her table. He had a girl with him. She had dark hair like Caleb. Caleb was dressed well, not his normal jeans and tee-shirt. The girl had on a dress and ballerina flats. She was tall and lean. Rayne recognized her from Caleb's usual gang.

Janie was watching Rayne as Caleb walked up. Janie and Sarah worked together trying to get Caleb to come. Sarah found him in the library during the week, she hid the secret from Rayne. Janie watched as her daughter's face lit up. He walked straight to Janie and Tom and shook their hands while he introduced himself and his guest. Her name was Selena and he introduced her as his sister. That was when Rayne noticed there might be similarities in their looks. She smiled at Selena when she came to sit next to her.

Once Caleb arrived, Rayne's dinner celebration passed quickly and comfortably. She could not have asked for a better night. Everyone got along and Caleb seemed to be charming the whole table. He was not the Caleb she was used to. He was almost manipulating in projecting himself as a charismatic, outward person when in fact Rayne knew otherwise.

As dinner started to wind down, Caleb asked Rayne's parents if she would be allowed to go with him and his sister for a bit after dinner. Janie could see Rayne's face light up and her dad Tom huffed at the idea. "I understand if you aren't comfortable with it but she will be perfectly safe. I promise." Caleb looked in Tom's eyes as he spoke to reassure him.

Janie nudged her elbow into Tom's arm and gave him a look with a slight nod to say yes. "Okay fine but only for two hours and no more than that or never again." Janie put her head on Tom's shoulder to show affection and gratitude for saying yes. Janie knew Rayne liked Caleb. She could see it in her face.

Everyone gathered outside to say goodbye and Tom reminded them of his two hour time limit. Rayne gave her guests hugs while she thanked them. Caleb shook her parents' hands and thanked them for dinner and letting Rayne go with him.

Caleb walked the girls to an old Volkswagen bus and opened the doors for them. Selena climbed in back and gave Rayne the front seat. "I didn't know you had a bus." Rayne shot a smug grin at Caleb as he closed the door for her. When he got in his seat he responded to her. "Well now you do." His white smile gleamed at her. He liked having her in his passenger seat.

She recognized the direction they were going, toward his camp. As they neared the spot he would usually turn into, he drove past it. They arrived to the top of the hill and he pulled over. He jumped out and went around and opened the girls' doors. "Why are we here?" Rayne was puzzled. They were on a hill overlooking the city and lake.

"I just want to show you this before we start our night." He took Rayne by her hand and walked her to the edge. She was flanked on both sides by Caleb and Selena. The three stared over the side and down at the glowing lights. It was a spectacular view. Rayne felt peaceful which was when she started to hear a hum in hear head, it was soft and melodic. As the volume rose, the city seemed to shine brighter with different colored hues. Rayne started to notice a change in her mood. She had become anxious and irritated.

The hum she was hearing had turned into Caleb's voice. "Rayne you need to relax. I'm here to help you."

Rayne did not understand what Caleb was supposed to help her with. She thought to herself, "Help me what?"

Caleb responded. "Help you to understand."

Rayne shifted her gaze to Caleb and looked at him puzzled. "You hear me?" Rayne's thoughts were still in her mind.

"Yes I hear you and I sense your tension. You have to learn to control that." His eyes were warm with concern.

"Control what? What's going on?" Rayne was only getting more frustrated. She had heard the voices before, but she thought her imagination was simply getting away from her. Now she was standing in front of Caleb hearing his voice as dread washed over her realizing it was not her imagination. Selena looked over at Rayne and walked back to the car.

Caleb opened his mouth to talk now. "I know this is a lot to take in right now but it's time you learned. The first thing is why we can hear our thoughts. Rayne there will be times when it is important that we can hear each other even if we are far apart. Selena can hear your thoughts too, the whole tribe can but we don't always communicate this way because it requires a lot of energy."

Rayne stopped looking at Caleb and started staring back down on the town. The colors were still there and she felt anger and frustration melt over her. She was not sure if it was because of what Caleb was telling her. She became more interested in absorbing the lights from the glowing town.

"Rayne, this is the other thing I need to tell you. The colors you see are people, but more specifically, their energy or what people call their aura. Most are peaceful and kind but the red you see and feel, those are people of threat." Caleb tried to read her but she spoke aloud.

"Aura? That's just fun and games, reading peoples aura. There's no such thing. Besides, it isn't just red. It's a red-black kind of glow." She was tense and now completely irritated as she spoke.

"No Rayne, the aura and energy you see is very real. It's the one thing people can't hide, not from us. Red can be seen many ways but our people know the bad red. Its energy is toxic until we extinguish it. I don't know about your red-black color but I know how you feel when you see it, that's why I am here to help."

"Extinguish it? This is amazingly surreal. Do you hear what you're telling me? Caleb how am I supposed to believe any of this?"

"I know if I were you I wouldn't believe it myself, but this is all real Rayne. You can see the colors, isn't that enough proof? There's more, but I think for now, you've heard enough. We need to go to camp for a bit." He put his arm around her shoulder and tried to guide her to the bus.

"Wait, why do we need to go to camp? I won't make it home in time."

"Don't worry I'll get you home on time. You'll feel better after we go to camp trust me please."

Rayne wanted to trust him but she was still hesitant. Finally, she begrudgingly got into his bus. Selena put her hand on Rayne's shoulder for moral support. They drove a little down the hill to where Caleb needed to park. They walked the path to the camp and as they entered, Rayne heard their humming. She felt the peace and began to relax. They joined everyone by the fire. As Rayne sat she relaxed, just as she had done the last time. Sleep blanketed her and the hum remained. Again, just like the last time, she felt the peace give way to many voices and confusion then suddenly quiet.

Once the quiet came she awoke to the tribe watching her. She looked around in embarrassment but they tried to ease her with the hum. Without words they wanted to let her know she should not be embarrassed. There was a sense of pride they tried to convey to her. She accepted it and as she did they all smiled at her. What her conscience mind did not know was that each time she had succumb to the trance, the family had given her a soul as she slept. They were helping to heal her.

It was time for Caleb to get her back home. Their ride was quiet. Caleb walked her to the door when they arrived. Still they were silent. He stared into her eyes and brushed his forefinger under her chin then he finally spoke. "You need some rest. I'll see you tomorrow." She went breathless when he touched her. He opened her door and guided her inside then closed the door behind her

Chapter 17

Learning a Piece of the Truth

The sun was squeezing though a crack in Rayne's blinds, otherwise she would have slept through the morning. Her sleep was restful and uneventful. Her parents were finishing up their breakfast when she walked into the kitchen. "You went right to bed when you got home. Did you have fun? Where did you kids go after dinner?" Rayne had no problem answering her dad's questions.

"Caleb and Selena wanted to take me to the overlook so we could see the city lights. I was tired when I got home so I went to bed. Sorry I didn't check in but I think I got home before my curfew."

"You did. We checked in on you but you were asleep. We tried to say goodnight and you didn't budge."

"Yeah I was exhausted. Trying to get everything lined up for graduation is wearing me out. I'm sorry I didn't say goodnight." Rayne sat at the table with her bowl of cereal.

"It's okay. We understand and like I said, you were home on time." Her dad lowered his newspaper as he spoke to her.

Janie chimed in. "So what are your plans for today?" The dishes clanged as she washed them.

"I'm not sure. Caleb said he'd be coming over but didn't say if we were doing anything. Why do you ask?"

"I was just curious. No reason. Should I make you two lunch or something?" Janie had a sweet shift in her voice.

"I don't know mom I'd hate for you to make something if he's made plans. I guess maybe sandwiches would be okay and if we don't eat them I can eat them for dinner. Heck, I don't even know if he's really going to come anyway." Rayne took her bowl to the sink to rinse it. "I'm going to get cleaned up now just in case he does come… although I'm not even sure when he'll be here." Rayne walked away rambling.

Janie and Tom talked about their daughter and her friend when she was out of earshot. Tom was worried but Janie was happy. He was being the typical protective dad and Janie the excited mom. Because Rayne had never shown any interest in boys, Tom never had to approach the idea of his daughter in a relationship. Now Caleb was in the picture. Tom's only comfort was that Rayne seemed to be dismissive about their relationship so he was not worried that she had a love interest in the boy.

It was noon when Caleb knocked on the door. Tom answered and Caleb extended his hand to greet him with a handshake while Tom reciprocated and asked him to come in. They sat in the living room together and Tom tried to find something they could talk about but Caleb only responded with short answers. Caleb was not interested in sports, current events or school. Trying to pry conversation out of Caleb only made Tom more unsettled about his daughter befriending him. His one hope was that she was using her best judgment with their friendship.

Just when things had gotten uncomfortably quiet, Rayne entered the room. "Hi. Sorry I wasn't ready when you got here."

"No worries your dad kept me entertained." He smiled and looked at Tom. Tom barely looked up at him.

"I'm not sure what you had planned but my mom said she'd make us lunch if you'd like."

Caleb agreed to lunch but asked if she wanted to go for a walk first. Rayne let her mom know they would be back to eat then they walked out the door.

During the first part of their walk they exchanged small talk. Caleb asked her how her sleep was and how she felt about the tribe. She told him she had not thought about it much until he mentioned it. She was feeling peaceful and clear with almost no thought. "I can tell you feel better. I feel it." He smiled and looked down on her as he talked.

"I don't understand this still. Why can I hear your thoughts? Why can you feel me? That just sounds creepy and unreal to say. Caleb, are you ever going to fill me in with what's going on?" Rayne could not begin to speculate what was happening inside her.

"I'm giving you time. It's hard not to tell you everything right now, but honestly I don't think you can handle it." He squeezed both of her shoulders softly. She still seemed relaxed and un-irritated at the situation.

"Is there anything I should be worried about? You realize how strange this sounds don't you?" She tilted her head as she looked up at him.

"No there's nothing to worry about, we'll take care of you. We have so far." He grabbed her hand and started to lead her home.

"See that makes me worry. Why do I need to be taken care of?" She tugged back on his hand a bit and slowed their pace.

"Everybody needs to be taken care of. Besides, I told you I'll tell you later. Just don't worry." He squeezed her hand and pulled her toward him.

She decided not to respond because she had come to the conclusion that he would keep telling her not to worry, unfortunately it was too late for that. They went back to her house and her mom had lunch ready.

Caleb had perfect manners while he ate his sandwich. All four sat at the table and struggled to break the awkward silence while they ate. Rayne's dad brought up a topic he was sure would get a conversation going. "So Caleb what are your plans after high school?"

Rayne looked at him with panic. She had not told her parents much about Caleb or his family. He did not hesitate to respond "Well Sir to be honest I'll probably stick with the family business. We are generations of carpenters and usually it's expected of us to follow."

"Well that's a noble trade and the world can't run out of things to build. What's the name of your family's company, if you don't mind my asking?" Tom was mindful of being respectful as he probed Caleb.

"Cheney Construction. It's a small company, we don't even have business cards but we get by." Caleb made sure to keep eye contact as he spoke. Rayne was surprised at the whole situation. Even she did not know the company name or Caleb's last name for that matter. She was now guessing it was Cheney.

"Cheney, that's Native American if I'm correct." Again, Tom remained courteous.

"Yes. A good number of my family is Native American but like the rest of the world, we have a varied family tree and generations of mixed races and ethnicities." Caleb must have practiced for this visit because he was on top of his game. He had gone head to head with Rayne's father and was impressive. Tom, himself, was finally feeling relaxed and started to soften up. As much as he tried not to like Caleb he found himself enjoying their conversation.

They all finished their meal and talked for another hour. Tom was laughing and lighthearted when they were done. Caleb surprised Rayne when he asked Tom if Rayne could go out with him for a bit. She was more shocked when her dad did not hesitate to say yes.

Caleb told Rayne to get a sweater as they told her parents goodbye. After the two left, Tom and Janie talked a bit more about Caleb. He mentioned how his first impressions were way off the mark and that Caleb was pleasant and Rayne really seemed happy with him. Janie was happy that Tom was warming up to him because she already decided she liked him.

Chapter 18

Rayne's Turn

Caleb took Rayne up to the area where his camp was but they took another trail off the opposite way. They walked through the woods, and for a while they listened to its sounds. The breeze shifted the leaves causing nuts to fall and ping around as they succumb to gravity and drop to the forest floor.

They moved deeper into the forest. Caleb carefully slid his hand down Rayne's forearm as he made his way to her hand. He softly gripped her fingers between his and Rayne's skin danced with excitement. They walked a bit farther before Caleb finally spoke. "Rayne, it's time you learned more. I don't know if you're ready, I don't know if you'll ever be, but it's time you knew."

Rayne was still tingling from his touch. "I'm ready, I'll be fine. I don't know what you're so worried about."

"Rayne, I already told you about feeling people and seeing their colors. You might not understand it but you've felt it a few times already. We've helped you control your anger. That's almost the hardest part because believe me, sometimes the urge is nearly uncontrollable."

"Yes, you told me all of that. I still don't understand."

"Well if you'd let me talk I'll try to find the words to make you understand. We've never had to explain this to anyone before. You're the first. That's what's taking so long. We've all tried to decide how to confront this."

"I'm really getting tired of this vague situation. If you could only hear it from my ears, you'd understand my confusion." She took her hand from Caleb. She was getting incredibly frustrated.

"I know and I'm sorry. Give me a minute, you might still be a little confused after I tell you, but at least you'll have a better understanding. Now don't interrupt." They stopped and sat on a rotting log.

Caleb went on to tell Rayne about his people and their place in the world. "We are different but you've been to my camp so you know that. My people see the bad in others. We know those that have dark in their souls, those that can't or don't have any intentions on changing, those with no hope or good in them. Our primary mission in life is to relieve them from this world and this life their souls have subjected them to. It is with their souls that we make our way to what you call heaven. Unfortunately, our methods are not conventional. It is because of our methods that you are how you are now. I was getting my breath and you happened to cross my path at the wrong time."

Rayne cut him off. "Wait a minute, wait a minute, who are you? You relieve people from this world? I still don't understand any of this." Her stomach started to ache.

"The night you got hurt and ended up in the hospital, I took you there. You were heading toward a group of homeless people along the road but you'd gotten there just when we were about to abolish a dark soul. I was two seconds away from him and you blocked his path, that's how you got hit. I barely started taking your breath when I realized it was you. Half a second in, anymore could've killed both of us. I took you to my family for a day to heal, then realized you had people looking for you. That was when I rushed you to the hospital. They thought you got hit by the car when I dropped you off, it's the story I decided to stick with."

"I remember passing out blankets that night. I remember everything right before the accident. Sarah was waiting in the car as I brought a load to a new group of men. I was walking toward them then all of the sudden I was hit with black. The next thing I remember was waking up in the hospital. All of that was because of you? I could have died? Until now, I did think I was hit by a car." Rayne was whirling in disgust with this new information. She noticed that the sun had dropped quickly and had a sudden desire to go home. Just then, there were crows lined in the branches above them. A few of them cawed and Caleb quickly stood up and pulled Rayne to her feet.

"We have to go." He pulled her behind him as he hurried through the path that led them back to his camp. She ran hesitantly. When they got there the fire was crackling and they were all sitting around humming. They looked toward Rayne and Caleb when they arrived. Rayne inhaled the soothing smell of burning sage and pine. The two sat with the others at the fire. Rayne was compelled to remain quiet. After a short time there was a group of them that stood. Caleb and Selena were part of the group. Caleb put his hand out for Rayne and she got up reluctantly. This was new for her. Usually during the fire gathering she was put to sleep. There was a soft humming in her head as she walked with them towards the tree line. The coyotes were gathered before them. Caleb and the group walked past the coyotes and they all picked up their pace. The animals stayed close behind.

As they neared the street their pace quickened. Rayne felt confusion as she moved with them. Suddenly they spread out and Rayne was with running with Caleb and two coyotes. There was a quick moment when clarity and focus pierced Rayne. She saw in the dark as Caleb swooped on a man, held him up to his mouth then as briefly as he held him, he tossed him under an oncoming car.

Rayne froze. She was paralyzed by the grotesque act. Her thoughts slammed her with grief, anger, and disgust. How could this sweet boy be so vile? He was just talking about how he is here to help relieve the dark from the bad people of this world when he himself was that dark person he spoke of.

When Rayne came to her senses, she turned and ran. She reached the street and ran in the direction of her house. She heard a coyote bark close behind her, then another. They were in unison. It was the same sound they had made when they were on the hunt. Rayne's feet were barely touching the ground as she picked up speed. She could feel herself run faster than she ever had. She was not athletic and never liked to run, but now she felt she was running for her life. She was barely outrunning the coyotes when she was abruptly swooped into a small tree grove. She had no time to think before she was pummeled to the ground.

Her hands were flailing until Caleb finally got control of them. "Rayne will you stop please!" She let out a scream and he pinned her hand down so he could free one of his hands to cover her mouth. "Rayne please be quiet. Let me explain." She still tried to scream through his fingers. "Please Rayne!" He rested his forehead on hers. His breath was coming out fast and in time with hers. "Please Rayne, let me explain." His voice was soft and pleading.

Rayne calmed down as a relaxed feeling came over her. "Are you going to let me talk now?" She hesitated before she shook her head yes. "What you saw, I've been trying to tell you about that but I just didn't know how to put it into words. You had to see to know, to understand."

"I saw, and what I witnessed was horrible. I don't understand it, how could you think I would? That was disgusting Caleb! You killed a man! Caleb you threw him under a car!" Rayne was irate when she responded.

"There is more to what you saw Rayne. That man, you saw his color I know you did. If you could only see what he's done you would understand. Rayne what I did was saved him from himself and anyone else he could hurt."

"I didn't see any saving. I saw killing! Caleb I witnessed a murder! You murdered a man! Why, because he was homeless? Because he was a drug user!" Rayne was furious.

"Rayne if that were his only faults he wouldn't have that light around him. Homelessness, drugs, alcohol, those are temporary predicaments that can be helped. What that man suffered from can't be helped here on earth. I know one day you will understand. I'm sorry that you have to go through this to learn the truth. I've been told that, for you, this will be the most painful part." Caleb was sorry. He wanted to hold her. He was in her head. He could feel her anger and hurt. Her eyes were fixed on his and she could feel his breath. As he moved his hand from her arms he brushed her chin with his fingers. She tried to fight it, but she was excited with his touch.

Annoyed with her inner struggle of pain and pleasure she smothered the excitement she had felt for Caleb and focused on the anger. "It's late and I'm sure my parents are worried. I need you to take me home now." She made sure to show no emotion. She did not realize Caleb could feel what she was not showing. He felt her excitement. It was a feeling he had never experienced before. His entire life had been about not feeling, only about doing.

"I'll get you home right away. I can't say sorry enough. If your parents are upset maybe I can talk to them." Caleb was as confused about what was going on with him as much as Rayne was about herself.

Rayne got up and brushed herself off. Caleb took her hand and led her to his van. It was parked closer than camp. He unlocked and opened her door then closed it behind her. She avoided making eye contact and resisted taking his hand when he took hers. She was irritated with herself, that she still found him attractive after what he had done. She tried to remember the first time she had seen him. She could not remember if she was drawn to him then, but she knew she was now.

Her phone had one missed call and two missed texts. It was her parents and before she could let them know she was safe, Caleb was nearly in her driveway. He walked her to the door and waited as she opened it. He wanted to be there if she needed him to talk to her parents. She was abrupt, "Don't worry. If they're upset I'll tell them we just lost track of time. You can go now." He did not want to go but he was not going to stand at the door and argue with her.

"I will come to see you tomorrow." He did not give her the option to answer.

When she went inside both Tom and Janie were prepared with a line of questioning. Rayne did just as she said and told them they had lost track of time and she enjoyed her time with his family. Rayne did not tell them that his family lived in a campground and she knew she could most certainly never tell them what he or his family did.

Rayne was not hungry for dinner and she told her parents she was tired and wanted to go to bed early. She barely put her head on the pillow when she dozed off and slept until morning. When she, awoke she still felt tired and had no appetite.

After she had been up for an hour Caleb came knocking on her door. She was not up for a visit and had no plans on getting out of her pajamas. She answered the door looking a mess and told Caleb she was staying in for the day. "Rayne we really need to talk. Can you come out for a little bit?"

"No Caleb, I'm tired and not in the mood." She leaned on the edge of the door as she spoke.

"That's what I need to talk to you about." He tried to keep her eyes on his. He could feel how tired she was.

"We can talk later, I really need some rest. Yesterday wore me out." Rayne gave him a smug look. Just then her dad came to the door to make sure everything was okay.

"What's up you two?" Tom sounded peppy as he spoke.

"Nothing dad. Caleb just came by to say hi" Rayne's tone was flat.

"Good morning Sir. I was hoping I could get Rayne to come out for a walk." He smiled as he spoke to Tom.

"From the looks of it, she's not feeling it today. Good to see you again, Caleb." Tom walked off.

"I'll talk to you later Caleb." Rayne was tired.

"But Rayne we really need to talk."

"Later this week okay." Rayne closed the door on him.

Caleb walked away defeated. Rayne's health was at risk. He did not want to alarm her but he knew sooner rather than later, she would need to go with him. He needed to convince Rayne but more than that, he wanted to be with her.

Rayne went back into the kitchen with her parents. Her dad was reading the Sunday paper and shared some of the stories. The one story Rayne managed to tune into was about a homeless man that staggered into an oncoming car close to their home. Rayne knew the real story. She was part of the real story. Her stomach knotted up as she listened. "I think I'm going to lay down for a bit. I'm still kind of tired."

Janie was concerned. "Are you feeling okay?"

"Yeah I just didn't get enough sleep." Rayne went to her room and took her textbooks to bed with her thinking she could get some studying in while she relaxed. It was getting close to finals and her head had not been focused on school work, especially economics. She disliked her teacher more than she did the actual class. He had a way about him that made her uncomfortable.

She rested and studied the remainder of the day only coming out for dinner and her shower. After her shower she told her parents good night and went to sleep. Her sleep was solid, just as it had been the night before.

Chapter 19

Rayne's Rage

Although she had a full night sleep, Rayne was tired again. She barely had the energy or desire to eat. Once again, Janie asked her if she was feeling okay. She told her she looked piqued and thought maybe she needed to stay home. Rayne told her it was too close to school being over for her to start staying home. She let her mom know that she would be fine once she got outside. Rayne nibbled on a breakfast bar and grabbed her backpack as she left. Janie hollered for her to call if she started feeling worse. "I'll be fine mom, but I'll call if I need to. Love you."

The air was comfortable. Rayne did not notice as she got to her car, there were crows lining the trees around her house. She piled her stuff into her car and when she backed out of her driveway she finally looked up and saw that she had an audience of crows surrounding her house. She looked around to see if she could see any coyotes or if Caleb was there, but she saw nothing.

On her drive to school she yawned numerous times. She was exhausted. She did not have to pick up Sarah because Scott was driving her now. Sarah usually would help to perk her up but now she had to entertain herself.

When she pulled into the school parking lot Scott and Sarah were already there. The three met up and walked together. As they walked, they made their usual plans to meet for lunch. Sarah asked Rayne if she was okay because she had looked tired. Rayne reassured her she was fine. They went off to their classes and as she walked, Rayne noticed the crows were along the telephone wires and in the tree branches. She still felt fatigued and barely made it through her classes. She was looking forward to her lunch with Sarah and Scott.

Her last class before lunch was her least favorite and her grade was evident of that. It was Economics with Mr. Louderbach. It was not that she was academically weak in the class, it was her lack of interest because her teacher made her uneasy. She noticed that he irritated her more, and now he had a red-black glow around him. It was the same thing she had noticed with other people lately, especially while she was tired. The aura's Caleb tried to tell her about.

There were things she needed to make up in his class and he suggested she stay in during lunch to catch up. She had texted Sarah to let her know she would not be at lunch. The bell rang and the classroom cleared out quickly. Rayne was the only one that Mr. Louderbach kept after class. He closed his blinds because the sun was shining through on the class.

She sat through fifteen minutes of his lunch time lesson before she noticed he was glowing redder. He had gotten close to her desk and started to lean over her shoulder and rub his leg on her. He slowly bushed his hand up her arm then slid across her back as he touched her. She could hear the crows outside cawing. Her blood was boiling as it pulsed through her veins. Her ears started ringing when he squatted down next to her. As she turned to look at him, he was bright red. He leaned into her face and she took both of her hands and placed them on his ears. She pulled his face into hers and with her lips barely scathing his, she inhaled. Her lungs were full of his life and as she breathed in, a quick flash of horrible things that he had done rushed through her. She had seen him with young girls, taking advantage of them and she sensed the joy he had gotten out of it. He was disgusting. She was repulsed by his delight and when he fell limp on the floor, a whirling relief encompassed her. She had done something she was compelled to do, and now she had an amazing sense of energy and famine.

While she tried to confront her confusion, Caleb burst into the classroom. "Rayne! What happened?" He knew he did not need to ask. He knew what had happened. "Rayne we need to call the school nurse. You tell her that he just collapsed. Call her now!"

Rayne did what Caleb told her. Within minutes the nurse was in the classroom checking Mr. Louderbach's pulse. She ordered Rayne to call 911. When Rayne reached the operator she told them that her teacher had collapsed and was told by the nurse to call. When the paramedics arrived they announced him deceased. Rayne was questioned and she told them that he was at her desk helping her with her work when he just fell to the floor. When the report was written they suggested he had a heart attack. Rayne was fine with that.

She had no remorse for the man. His soul was dark. He was gone and could no longer hurt anyone. Rayne was fine with that too. What she did have difficulty with was trying to understand who she had become.

The school excused Rayne for the remainder of the day. They told her parents that they thought the incident might be traumatic for her. Caleb drove her home in her car. Her parents were not home from work yet. He decided to take the opportunity to finish telling Rayne what she needed to know.

He told her about how unique their kind was and that Rayne was rarer than the rest. He reminded her that she should have died the night of the accident and since then, the tribe had been trying to figure out how to handle her.

Rayne still could not grasp the concept so Caleb decided to tell her about his journey with hopes that it would enlighten her. He told her he was born barely over a hundred years ago, before technology could be imagined. His parents were mixed Native American and Irish, which was not completely common during that time. The town they lived in was Bend, located in Oregon. The population was sparse and most kept to themselves.

At an early age Caleb seemed different and an aunt of his noticed. This aunt told Caleb's mom Ana, about a special part of the family's ancestry. Random generations produced a child that was born to help humanity. The child grows at a normal rate until they end their toddler years, then they age according to their journey. These people were called Soul

Collectors, and for centuries, they were tasked to take the souls of the morally corrupt.

When the children are born they appear quite normal. When they enter toddler years they

show signs of their gift. Unfortunately, those indications appear as aggressive tantrums

that are nearly uncontrollable without the proper supervision. At adolescence, they are

fully immersed in a new tribe consisting completely of their kind and governed by a

higher court of elders.

Caleb was brought to the tribal council when he was four and he had been with his new

family since. They work together to prepare a child for what they are to do in life. Caleb

told Rayne that he happened to be a particularly unruly child and more difficult than most

to teach. He nearly exposed his people when he took it upon himself to take a soul in

public. It was easy to cover up the incident in the early days because technology and

population did not interfere. He had not made another mistake until Rayne came along.

Rayne cut in, "Tribe, so you *are* all Native American?" She was not anymore clear on

who he was but he had kept saying tribe, which led her to believe they were all Native.

"No actually, not at all. We are from all parts of the world and we generally stay in the

region we're from. It's easier when we know the cultures and what's considered

acceptable norms." His face stayed straight as he talked. It was important to him that

Rayne understood what he was teaching her.

"Then why do you keep saying you're in a tribe and your people?"

"We are a tribe. We could say clan or gang but everything has a connotation and tribe is most suitable for us. We are a group of people. Not unlike any other group of people, only we have a special gift that isn't acceptable to any society."

"Yeah, you kill people." She rolled her eyes, still not convinced that he was anything but bad.

Caleb still could not find the right words and his story was not helping to change her mind. "Rayne, you go to church right? Do you think everyone in your church is good? Do you think your tribe of people has only good intentions? What about your teachers? You obviously know how that turns out. Law enforcement and soldiers, do you think they all have good intentions? Rayne there are dark people everywhere and they hide behind a façade of uniforms, education, and faith. Before the accident, you could not see them. You walked among them like everyone else, ignorant to their evil. The only time you learned about them was when it was too late, when they became a violent or a perverse news story. Those people you see now, they won't change. Their desires can't be controlled until they hurt someone. Rayne they're rapists and murders not drug users or thieves. It isn't an illness that makes them that way, it's their own ugly desires and demons. They can't be helped, unlike thieves or addicts. We help them by taking away their painful souls. We take away what drives them and hurts others."

Rayne remembered the day in church when she could barely stand to sit in her seat. She had seen a few people that had a red aura around them. She felt infuriated and almost could not contain herself. It was the same thing she had seen with her teacher before she took his soul. During her recollection, she started to understand. She did not feel that she had killed the man, but she still felt indignant with the situation. "Okay, I get it. Well I'm trying to get it, but I don't understand how it's right?"

"Anyone who isn't one of us won't understand. If we don't take their malicious souls, we won't live. It's our life source, and believe me it pains me to say this, but there is plenty of life source in this world. So many dark people are here hiding in plain sight. Rayne they need us to do our work here. I'm sorry you've been taken like this. I'm sorry you are being forced to understand something no one of your kind could possibly fathom but it's happened and you can't go back. You are now our kind." Caleb's expression softened.

"What do you mean I can't go back? I'm not going anywhere no matter what's happened to me. My parents are going to flip Caleb!"

"What I mean is you can't go back to being who you were and eventually you will have to come to our family. It's just how things are done. There is no other way. Oh, and you can't tell your parents." Caleb stood up. He wanted to be gone before her parents got home.

"Are you kidding me? Is there some master plan I'm missing here? Caleb you've only known me for a short time but you can imagine this isn't going to work out how your people think it's going to. I don't care 'how things are done'." Rayne stood up and was almost in his face.

"Rayne you're eighteen and legally an adult. You can make your own choices now. You're parents have no say. And no we don't have a master plan. Like I told you this hasn't happened before." Caleb walked toward the door. "I'll talk to you later." He knew she would be fine now that she had gotten the energy she needed from taking her teacher.

"Caleb, you can't just leave!" Rayne ran to the door.

"Rayne you'll be fine. We'll talk later." He walked away as she stood at the door.

Her parents had come home early and barely missed Caleb. They were worried about Rayne after the school called them about what had happened. When Janie walked in, she made sure Rayne had not been traumatized and afterward she noted how well Rayne looked considering the circumstances.

Rayne did feel good. She felt rested and hungry. After she mentioned being hungry Janie was in the kitchen whipping something up for her. Lately her mom was worried about her because Rayne had been exhausted and had no desire to eat. After she ate everything on her plate she requested more and when she was done she told her mom that she wanted to go to the library to catch up on work she missed because she left school early.

"Are you sure you want to go, Rayne? I'm guessing the school is going to give you a little break on your work considering the circumstances."

Rayne was not worried about doing her work. She was hoping Caleb might follow her there. "I know mom but I really feel like getting out. I'm fine." She was fine. There was no love loss with her teacher. She had no remorse for taking his life.

"Fine. Go, but keep your phone with you in case you need me."

"Of course mom, I always do."

Rayne drove to the library and noticed there were no crows and at the library, there was no Caleb. She stayed for over two hours and nothing. She gave up hope and went home.

Chapter 20

New Adjustments

The week passed and Rayne did not see Caleb or his family. During school she noticed the other kids glancing at her but trying not to stare. There were whispers about her teacher and everyone shared a sense of concern and compassion for Rayne. Her senior year had been news worthy, starting with her accident and ending with her teacher falling dead right in front of her, of course by her hand. No one was the wiser, other than Caleb.

As each day passed, Rayne tuned out her classmates more. She noticed that each of them had their own aura. While Rayne felt rested, she noticed that they were more faint than the day she took her teachers soul.

She had gone to church with her parents and noticed just as she did the last time, everyone's glow. It was not as bright as the first time she witnessed it but she definitely saw them. There were a few that were muted red-black, but she knew that soon enough they would illuminate as bright as a red bulb.

She recognized a few of them. One was a police officer that had befriended her parents. Rayne was not feeling disgust for him yet, she just knew he had grievous intentions. She was in complete control as she scanned the congregation. If they only knew what she could see while those that were benevolent stood shaking hands with those that were malevolent.

"Rayne are you okay?" Janie gently elbowed her daughter to get her respond. "Officer Bradley is talking to you."

"Oh I'm sorry. I guess I was lost in thought. Hello officer. What was it you were saying?" Rayne plastered a fake smile on as she responded.

"I was asking if you're ready to graduate. You're a senior this year if I remember correctly." He was charming and overly attractive.

"Yeah I guess I'm ready. I really didn't know what to expect and well, it's been a crazy year." Rayne still had her fake face on.

"I was one of the responders to your school. Sorry to hear about that. I would have come to check on you but another officer got your report."

Rayne was happy he was not the officer that helped her. She was not sure what she would have done. She still had no real clue to what drives her or her new abilities. "I'm okay, I was just a little shaken that day. It's sad that it happened, but I'm sure he's in a better place now." Rayne was not sure if he *was* in a better place but she knew no matter where he was, her teacher could no longer hurt anyone.

The family finished their Sunday and by the time Rayne went to bed, she wondered when she would see Caleb again. She had started to miss him in a different way. She missed his family as well.

As each day passed, she felt emptier and by midweek she felt vacant. Lethargy had started to set in again and as everyone around her started to shine a little brighter, she grew weary.

Thursday morning she did not want to get out of bed. When Janie checked on Rayne she noticed her skin was pale and she felt clammy. After the two argued about going to the doctor, Janie let Rayne have her way and stay in bed. She told her that if she were not better by the time she came home from work, they would head straight to the doctor. Rayne told Janie that she would try to eat something.

Janie made sure Rayne's phone was next to her in case she needed to call. She also asked her again if she wanted her to stay home with her. After Rayne reassured her that she would call if she got worse, Janie left for work.

As Rayne dozed off, she did not notice the crows had lined her tree branches outside. She had been asleep for over an hour when there was a sudden ruckus outside. The crows were cawing but Rayne did not have the energy to go see what they were having a fit about. Her eyes closed again but not for long. She awoke to Caleb shaking her. She was confused. She knew she was in her room but did not know how he got there. His voice sounded distant "Rayne… Rayne… You have to wake up! Rayne can you hear me?" She wanted to respond but she did not have the strength to get the words out.

He picked her up and carried her to his VW bus and laid her across his backseat. He rushed to his seat and sped off to his camp. As he pulled into the parking area, a few people from his family were there to greet him and help to carry Rayne to camp. Although it was daylight, there was a campfire burning. The whole family was seated around it and there was a blanket to lay Rayne on.

The hum was a low pitch and it seemed to sound almost pleading. The smoke from the fire floated slowly toward the sky. The volume of the hum grew as Rayne fell deeper into sleep. The energy around the ring was intense. There was an insistence about the hum and the fire.

It was daylight which made it riskier helping Rayne. There was light traffic on the highway as Caleb and his sister stood along the roadside. There was a small encampment close by that was nestled behind the tree line. Caleb knew there were at least two people in there that could help Rayne recover. Caleb and Selena stalked the site and positioned themselves for attack. It was a struggle to see their aura since they had already taken the souls they needed to live. Rayne was not there for the hunt which is why she was sick. She needed a black soul.

Caleb and Selena sat patiently and did not have to wait long for their lucky break. A burly older man appeared to walk away possibly to go to the bathroom. He would be hard for the two to carry but it needed to be done. As he stood burrowed in some shallow trees, he proceeded to relieve himself. That was when Caleb signaled Selena to move in. His aura was red but it was a dim red. They had to make sure that they only knocked him out. Rayne needed him alive so that she could live. With a stick that was thick enough to fit in his palm, Caleb swiftly swung and made contact with the base of the man's skull. He fell with a solid thud.

Both Caleb and Selena hoisted the man and cuffed their shoulders under his rancid armpits. He smelt foul and his pits were still wet with sweat. He was heavy as his legs dragged under his body. They went back around the way they came and were never detected.

There were no cars as they crossed the highway and nobody was hiking on their path back to the campsite. They could hear the humming long before they reached the camp. Rayne was lying lifeless on the blanket Caleb had placed her on. Their captive had become nearly unbearable to carry as they jogged the last few yards to Rayne.

When the man was placed on his side next to Rayne, the groups hum had turned into a chant. He was laid in a position that faced Rayne then they turned Rayne to face him. It was a short few minutes as the chanting grew louder, that Rayne uncontrollably and swiftly inhaled the stranger's soul. He did not suffer and passed in seconds. He was

Rayne's fourth soul since she had changed. Three of the souls were brought to her by the family.

Before she could stir, Caleb and Selena pulled the man back onto their shoulders and dragged back into the woods. They got him as far as the tree line on the other side of the highway and made sure to lay him down out of sight. By the time they returned to camp Rayne was sitting up with a blanket on her shoulders. One of the older family members was handing her a cup with steam coming out of it.

As Rayne sipped on her tea, Caleb sat next to her. She kept her eyes focused on the fire and she whispered thank you to him. They both sat listening to the low hum of the family and the crackle of the fire. After an hour Caleb told Rayne he needed to get her ready to go back home.

Rayne had only been gone a few hours but Caleb knew her mom would be worried. He helped Rayne to the front seat of his van. No one said a word as she walked through the camp.

He did not talk much during the drive. He warned her with few words that she needed to take care of herself or this would happen again and would keep happening. Rayne did not say anything. He walked her to the door and told her she needed to rest more. He opened the door and closed it behind her.

Chapter 21

SAT's

The house was quiet. Rayne had made it home before her mom. She went into her room and checked her cell phone. She missed six calls and three texts from her mom. In the texts Janie stated she started to worry because she was not responding. The last text she sent was only twenty minutes before Rayne got home and said that she was on her way home because Rayne was not responding to her calls. Just as she finished reading, the front door opened.

"Rayne" her mom said as she walked toward her bedroom.

"Yeah mom. I'm in my room." Rayne sounded healthy.

Janie walked in the door and saw that her daughter had color back in her cheeks as she sat up in her bed. "Why didn't you answer your phone? How are you feeling?"

"Oh sorry mom. I was sleeping and Caleb brought me some soup from his family. I think it helped. I was just going to text you back right before you came in the door."

"Caleb came by? That was nice. It looks like his soup worked. I might have to get the recipe."

"I'll tell him you thanked him." Rayne smiled at her mom.

"Do you need anything?" Janie still had her purse on her shoulder as she sat on Rayne's bedside.

"No mom, I think I'm fine for now. I'll get a little more rest so I can be ready for school."

Janie brushed Rayne's hair off her forehead and gave her a kiss on the space she cleared. The show of affection was also to check for fever. Janie was satisfied that her daughter finally did feel normal. "Rest sounds good. Let me know if you do need something."

"I will but I'm sure I'll be fine." She smiled at her mom and lay back down.

Rayne went back to school and managed to catch up on her missing work. During a dinner conversation, her dad asked her if she had gotten her paperwork done for community college and if she was ready for her SAT and end of year exams. Rayne reassured him that she was lining everything up for college and studying every day for her exams.

Rayne did not hear from Caleb for the next week and a half. She was distracted and focused on school. She was feeling healthy and at the same time she had become more in tune with her surroundings. The people around her were different or at least they seemed different. She could feel them, not read their minds but feel who they were inside similar to how an animal may sense the good or bad in a human.

Friday came and the family made plans to celebrate Rayne finishing finals and her SATs and would be graduation soon. They were going to dinner at a place a few towns over. It was a new place they had never been before but Rayne's mom heard good reviews about it. Rayne loved Italian food so she was really looking forward to it.

Rayne's parents invited her friends to come along but Rayne told them that Caleb declined. Caleb did not decline, truthfully Rayne had not heard from him. Janie had asked about Caleb but Rayne told her that she did not have much time to visit with him lately since she had been busy studying.

The weather was getting warmer but it was still cool enough in the evening to wear a light sweater. Rayne drove with her parents. There was a good size group by the time her friends and their parents had arrived. Rayne had noticed a new but familiar feeling. She started getting fatigued. Now that she started to recognize the link to her accident and what she seemed to become, the fatigue meant only one thing.

She knew she would have no problem enjoying her dinner. When the exhaustion starts, it comes on subtly, but that is when she starts to notice everyone's aura glow a little brighter. It was strange to her, but that made dinner more pleasant. Everyone illuminated so peacefully. Her parents glow was especially pleasing. As dinner passed, so did the time. Before the group realized it, they were the last patrons in the restaurant.

Rayne's parents said goodbye to everyone and were the last to pay their bill. They were getting ready to walk to their car when Rayne realized she left her sweater on the back of her chair. She told her parents that she would be right back out. Their car was at the end of the lot and the lighting was poor so her father told her that he would drive up to get her once they got the car.

It took a few minutes for Rayne to retrieve her sweater and as she exited the front doors, she noticed her parents had not started the car. She could barely see their glow but she did see something she had not expected. A bright red glow was standing on the passenger side of the car.

Rayne was stealth as she moved in toward the car. She felt furious and as she got closer she had every sense of the person standing next to her mother. She was nearly rabid has she approached them. In a swift motion she knocked the person to the ground and without thinking she took his breath. In seconds he was gone. Rayne was fueled as her mother stood screaming and her father ran to pull her off the man she had just killed.

"Rayne! Rayne! What are you doing?" Tom pulled Rayne up worried about her safety then tried to check the pulse on the man. There was none. Tom got up and hugged Rayne. He tried to understand what he had just seen. There was no way to describe it. Rayne did nothing but tackle the man and he had died from that. "We have to call the police." Tom pulled out his cell phone.

"No, dad don't." Rayne was focused now. "You can't call the police."

"Rayne this man is dead. It needs to be reported." Tom started to dial 911 and pulled Rayne over to her mom.

"Dad you can't." Rayne was insistent.

"Yes I can and I am." Tom reached the operator and told her his location and that there was a dead man.

Rayne was pacing. She tried to figure out what she needed to do. Caleb was not there to help her. How could she explain what had happened? Within a minute there was an officer in the lot with them. "Good evening folks, I'm Officer Johnson. Where is the man you called about?" Tom motioned to the direction of the man that was about to attack he and his wife. "How long has he been down?" Officer Johnson had his pad out as he started to jot down notes.

Tom looked at his watch. "I'd say about ten minutes."

"Can you tell me everything that occurred before he went down?" The officer was ready to hear the story.

Tom described every detail up to his daughter tackling the man. When Tom told the officer that his daughter responded impulsively by simply leaping toward him, she knocked him to the ground which is when he became unresponsive. Rayne managed to overhear her father and was relieved when he did not tell the officer the part about her literally inhaling the life out of him. She did not have to explain anything. She was halfheartedly consoling her mom.

Janie was still shaking. Rayne was not sure if it was because she barely escaped an attack, or if it was the fact that she witnessed her daughter take the man's life. Rayne knew she could not tell her parents what she had become.

They were still at the scene when the ambulance arrived to pick him up. Rayne overheard the officer tell the paramedic the story and suggested he may have passed due to head trauma or possibly natural causes. There were no weapons used. The officer said that the assailant did have drug paraphernalia on his person which may suggest another reason for his passing. The paramedic said cases like this usually go to the morgue and if warranted, the assailant would be autopsied.

After the officer was pleased with the contact information, he dismissed Rayne and her family. The drive home was quiet. Their perfect evening had become tarnished with death and now somehow Rayne would have to explain the unexplainable to her parents. But how could she explain something she knew virtually nothing about?

At home, Janie went straight to her room. Tom told Rayne that her mother was probably tired and shook up from the night. He gave Rayne a hug and told her to sleep well. Rayne was surprised when she woke up. She slept through the night. She might have slept through her morning if it were not for the ruckus outside of her window. She opened her blinds and saw a large family of crows strewn across tree limbs. As she looked down, she saw two coyotes sitting at the trunk of one of her trees. Rayne knew that with the coyotes, usually Caleb was near. She looked everywhere and did not see him. She had given up finding him after peering into every crevice he might be hiding in. Her stomach growled loudly. She did not realize how famished she was. Her parents were not up yet. It was not usual for Rayne to be up before her them and she did not give it much thought.

As she was pouring a bowl of cereal she heard a light tap on her back door. The tapping persisted. Rayne walked quietly to the door and waited to hear it one more time before she unbolted the lock. There was no peep hole so she could not look out to see who was on the other side. As she eased the door open she made sure to keep her foot nudged up on the bottom so that she could restrict it from opening too much. It was difficult for her to see anyone through the small crack she created. She tried to see as far as she could when Caleb's head abruptly popped into view.

"Rayne!" His voice was hushed but aggressive. "What have you done?"

Rayne stepped out onto her back porch. The cold air made her shiver and she stood in quiet as she tried to think of how to answer to Caleb. She knew exactly what he was talking about, she just did not know how to answer.

"What are you talking about Caleb?" The first thing that came to her mind was to act dumb about it.

"Rayne you know exactly what I'm talking about." He was so close to her face she could feel his breath.

It was obvious acting ignorant about the situation would not make it go away. "It just happened. I'm sorry. My mom was going to get hurt."

"Rayne, they saw you. How are you going to explain this to them? We don't just go around killing people in front of other people! There can't be any evidence of our kind." Caleb was furious. He had never showed anger like this before.

"I said I'm sorry. I just saw red. He wasn't a good man. When I took him I saw everything. I wasn't just defending my parents, I was... Well I don't know how to explain it. I felt... Ugh, I felt compelled to do it. I really don't understand this! Why... Why did I do it Caleb?" Although she did not understand why she had done it, Rayne did not feel bad for what she had done to the stranger. She had the same feeling she did when she took her teacher. However, she was emotionally weighed down by how it had affected her parents.

Caleb paced back and forth debating on how to handle the situation. The entire family knew what had happened and no one had an idea on what they were to do. Caleb wanted to go to the counsel and the family agreed. He was perplexed on forcing Rayne to go with him or to take the trip alone. Rayne had no idea about the counsel. To this point, she still had not been told enough to keep herself out of trouble.

"Rayne, you have to promise me you won't do this again. I have to leave for a bit and I won't be here to protect you. Don't say anything to your parents… Don't say anything to anybody!" Caleb was holding her shoulders as he implored her.

"I won't. Believe me, I wouldn't know what to say to them anyway. That's why I haven't talked yet. My mom is a mess from this. I think my dad is in denial about what he witnessed. When will you be back?"

"I don't know, maybe a little longer than a week. Seriously, stay out of trouble and don't tell anyone!"

"Okay, okay. I'll keep my mouth shut." She reassured Caleb once more before he ran away. She wanted him to stay. While he was with her, she felt normal. Until he had come to visit, she had been feeling like a monster, unsure and confused of who and what she was. While Caleb was there she had a calming sense of peace and understanding.

Rayne turned to walk back into her house and inside her head she heard "Don't worry Rayne, I will help you." It was Caleb's voice. She smiled.

Chapter 22

Caleb and Counsel

Caleb's family helped to pack him up for his trip. Selena would be going with him. They were driving to the White Mountains in Arizona to meet with the counsel. The counsel was a collection of the elder soul reapers and whenever any situation surfaced it was mandatory for a meeting with them.

The rest of the family would stay behind and keep an eye on Rayne. Caleb and Selena braced themselves for the long ride. It would take them at least a full day of driving to reach their destination.

The White Mountains were picturesque year round. The streams were full of trout and the trees and flowers were green and blooming. Caleb usually enjoyed his trips to see the elders, but this time was different. He was worried about what they may say.

Rayne had done something none of the soul reapers had ever done. She was witnessed taking a soul. Caleb did not know what the punishment would be. He and everyone in his family were taught, at their earliest ages, the importance of their secret. While the souls were often taken in public, there were never witnesses. Even when Caleb was a child and took his first soul, there were no witnesses. There had never been a need for punishment.

When the two pulled into the elders' camp, they were greeted with the sound of a soft hum and four gray-haired women. They kept their gear in the van and walked with the women. They were placed at the fire and situated across from the most powerful elder, the Superior. There was neither talking nor thought. The silence lasted thirty minutes. Finally the Superior's voice sounded in Caleb's head. "My son, I understand this problem. I understand your fear. It will not be easy to recover from the damage that has been done which is now my fear."

"I hear you Superior. What is it I am supposed to do?" They were communicating through thought. Their eyes fixed on each other.

"You've already started mending the problem. I have faith that you will work through it and do what you need to." After the superior spoke, Caleb was more confused than he was when he arrived. He had no idea what he needed to do. He always came to his leader for advice. This was the first time his trip deemed unhelpful.

Once the Superior delivered his last thoughts the hum started along the circle. Caleb knew that meant the conversation was over. He waited until he and his sister were served their food before he said anything to her. "Did you understand what Superior said?"

Selena waited to swallow her food before she responded. "What do you mean? I didn't hear a thing. What did he say?" Caleb and Selena were speaking in hushed voices.

"Never mind I probably just imagined it. I'm kind of tired from the drive." Caleb did not know why Selena did not hear what was spoken telepathically. This type of solitary communication had never happened as far back as he could remember. The Superiors message was usually heard by the entire family.

Shifting his thinking back to the problem at hand, he had to figure out what his leader meant. He did not know what he had already done to help or what else was he supposed to do. He wondered if he was supposed to get rid of Rayne or her family. He was at an impasse. It was not in their nature to hurt good people. That was not their mission in life. Innocent people were innocent no matter their accidental mistakes. If anything, Caleb made the mistake by changing Rayne. What Rayne did would not be considered a mistake if it were not for her parents seeing her. As he thought about it, he realized her parents were the problem, not Rayne. He could not wrap his mind around what he was to do.

Caleb and Selena slept before they prepared to drive back to California. As Caleb slept he dreamt of Rayne. He recalled the first night he had come in contact with her. The scene played out during his nocturnal state. It was rare for Caleb to dream but he could not stop this one. In his dream, he accounted for every moment he had known Rayne. He realized that he was the source of his problem, but that it was not a problem. He had been taking care of what he had done the whole time and Rayne's parents needed to see what she had become because Rayne could not go back to what she was, mortal.

Caleb's dream gave him a slight insight of his new journey but he also questioned if it was a dream. He woke and made sure to recall all that he had seen during his slumber. He was confused because what he now believed he was to do had never been done before. Telling mortals about his people was always against the rules. Now he was compelled. Rayne would die otherwise. He could not stand that thought.

Caleb met with Superior before he and Selena packed to go. "You now know what you are to do, my son?" Superior did not look at him as he spoke.

"I believe so, Superior." Caleb faced the Superior as he spoke.

"Follow your dream." The Superior did not move his mouth but sent his thought to Caleb and looked into his eyes as he did then he excused Caleb.

After the van was loaded, Caleb attempted to turn on the ignition. There was no sound. The van was dead. He tried the key again and still nothing. He lifted the hood and poked around to see if something had been disconnected. Caleb found the generator had gone bad. Days had passed when they finally got the generator that was needed to get him going.

Because of his van, Caleb had not seen Rayne in just over a week, and he knew that she was past due for a soul collection. He worried that she would do the same thing she had done the last time and risk getting caught again.

They drove the speed limit between Arizona and California. After stopping a few times for short breaks, they were home. Caleb immediately sensed something was wrong. He dropped Selena off at camp and sped over to Rayne's.

Chapter 23

Caleb Comes Home

He knocked on the door aggressively a few times. It took a few minutes for Janie to finally open the door. She looked pale and worried. "Hi Caleb. Rayne isn't feeling well. I'm afraid she isn't up for any visitors. I'll tell her you came by."

Janie started to close the door when Caleb gently stopped it from closing and asked her if he could see Rayne. "It might lift her spirits" he insisted.

"I don't think so. She's been sick for a few days and only getting worse. I'm not sure if what she has is contagious. Maybe in a few days. I really am sorry you wasted your time coming over." Janie was not going to let Caleb in.

"I might be able to help if you just let me see her. My family has helped her before." Caleb was trying to make his case.

"Caleb, I don't think she's been like this before. She's been sleeping for the last two days, and before that she wouldn't eat much. We are about to have a doctor come over because she is too weak to leave." Janie was getting irritated with Caleb. She wanted to be back at her daughters beside.

"A doctor can't help her. You need to let me in." He stepped toward the door, with Janie being irritated and now frustrated, he managed to break through her stronghold.

Rayne still let her empathy control her, which was one of the reasons she had gotten so ill. The other reason was her fear of getting caught or doing the deed haphazardly. Janie followed him to Rayne's bedroom. Caleb nearly fell apart when he saw Rayne. She was pale and sunken. There was no life in her face as she slept. He touched her cheek and her skin was cold. "You have to let me take her. I can help her."

Janie was not going to let him take her daughter. "Absolutely not! You've got to be kidding me! Do you see her? Why do you think I would let you take her? My child, my sick daughter! What mother in her right mind would let that happen?"

Caleb knew he was not going to convince Janie and he did not know how long Rayne had. It looked like she would not make it through the night and contrary to what her mother thought, a doctor would be of no help. Rayne was dying and Janie did not know it. Caleb tried to think of a way to get Rayne out of the house.

"You can come with me. Both of you." He looked at Janie and Tom. "She needs help now and I can help her." Caleb was not sure if it was a smart move asking her parents to come, but it was his only option.

Tom finally spoke. "Janie, I know this seems crazy and unbelievable and honestly I don't know why, but I think we have to say yes to this." Tom remembered the last time Rayne had gotten sick and after she spent time with Caleb she was back to herself. Tom had no idea what he did to help Rayne then but she needed help now, no matter what it was. His fears had him thinking that Caleb may have gotten her hooked on something but she was so sick that she needed help right away and Tom was hopeful that Caleb could help her. He decided he would let Caleb take care of her, then he and his wife would take over and help her to recover and remain healthy.

Caleb insisted that Rayne ride in his van so she would be able to lie down. Tom and Janie would follow in their car. They followed him to the road up the mountain. Rayne's dad did not know what to expect or where he was going. They parked along a tree line and Caleb had the two get in the van with them. Although he warned his camp, his family would not welcome a strange car coming to their camp.

As the van eased through the path, the crows lined the tree branches. The sun was setting and the silhouette of trees looked black as the amber sky pierced behind them. All was quiet, other than a few caws from the crows. The van stopped and when Caleb opened the doors, Tom and Janie peered out onto the small crowd of people looking at them in a peaceful silence. Before he pulled Rayne out of the backseat, the family started their enchanted humming.

Tom and Janie were led to a spot by the fire as their daughter was placed on a blanket next to them. After Caleb carefully set her down, he looked intently at both of her parents and stated vehemently that they needed to trust him and his family. He knew that what they were about to witness would have a profound effect on them. "I won't let anything happen to Rayne. We care about her. Our practice isn't traditional and there's a good possibility you may question it, but trust me we only wish her well." He lightly squeezed both of their arms hoping they would understand that this was his way of expressing compassion and empathy for their family. He never had to exude feelings like this before and although the feeling was foreign to him, it had almost felt comfortably natural.

They sat quietly as the hum grew louder. While the tranquil noise relaxed the two, the smoke from the fire put them in a sort of trance. Caleb and Selena knew this was the time for them to do their work. They had to travel farther down the road to collect the person that would heal Rayne. Their resources were becoming limited and more dangerous for them in their local area.

Two miles away there was a bar with a steady flow of degenerates. It was a good spot to find an out-of-towner that was up to no good. There were a number of motorcycles lined up outside and as the two looked in the door, it was easy to spot the few that had a red glow pulsing through the room. Since they had traveled to Arizona, Caleb and Selena had to go an extended period of time between collecting souls. This made them weak, but not too weak to help Rayne.

Caleb waited outside as Selena strolled into the bar. It was quick work for a stranger to make her acquaintance and true to form, he pulsed red. She went to the bathroom and walked past the stranger. Within minutes, the man was out the door trying to tail Selena down the road. He finally caught up to her on a dark spot along the street. There were not many street lights so it would be hard for the stranger to see that Caleb was following them. She did not want to carry the man far so she used the thoughts inside her head to communicate to Caleb that she was going to convince him to walk with her as far as she could get him to go. Caleb agreed and stayed back a safe distance.

Selena managed to get the stranger to walk a mile, but she could sense he did not want to wait any longer. It was not in this wicked man's nature to wait. He was dark and a mile was all he could take. He wanted her. She signaled Caleb that he needed to catch up and before she finished her thought, she heard the thud to his head before the man fell to the ground. Caleb had to make sure not to hit him too hard. He needed to be alive for Rayne.

The two lifted and carried the man the way someone would carry an inebriated person. Each had one arm over their shoulder. When they got back to camp they did the same thing they had done the last time Rayne needed help. They placed the stranger alongside Rayne and faced both towards each other. Rayne's parent's eyes were fixed on the fire. Caleb barely paid attention to the two because Rayne was his priority. He was not sure what was happening with Tom and Janie altogether. This was a new predicament and not one he or his family could have prepared for. Caleb could only assume there was a higher power helping them.

Within minutes, Rayne started to cough. The sound of her cough seemed to stir her parents. She started to sit up and her parents looked down at the man who was unconscious, or at least they thought he was unconscious. They had no idea what had occurred, they only witnessed that their daughter seemed to have some life in her now. Janie smiled with a tear in her eye and Tom hugged her. While the family was embracing each other, Caleb and Selena took advantage of the distraction and dragged the man off.

The two dragged the stranger back down to the area where they had found him. While they were gone, Tom and Janie tried to thank Caleb's family for the help. Caleb's family continued to hum and disregard Rayne's parent. Tom decided this was the opportunity to take their daughter back to their car and head home. Rayne seemed more than healthy enough to walk the distance to their car. Her parents were surprised as she led them through the dark forest, directly to the doors of their car.

The drive home was quiet. It was too much to make sense of and Rayne's parents were exhausted.

Chapter 24

Revelations

The next morning Rayne was starving. The family joined together at the table for breakfast, but before any conversation started, Rayne piled food on her plate. Both Janie and Tom watched as she nearly inhaled her food and went back for another plate.

Janie broke the silence by clearing her throat. Rayne looked up and finally spoke, "Good morning mom." Rayne smiled.

"So you're feeling better?" Janie muttered a bit as she spoke. She did not know whether to be angry or concerned about what had happened and the fact that within twenty-four hours, her daughter went from being nearly comatose to jubilant and ravenous.

"I am, thank you. What happened?" Rayne did not remember most of the night. She only became aware at the point when she was hugging her parents as Caleb's family watched. Rayne knew some form of conversation needed to happen about the strange things that had been happening but she did not know what she was allowed to say.

They both proceeded to tell her the details they recalled and what led up to it. Rayne knew she was sick and recalled when it was that she started to get sick. Days before she had become too weak to get out of bed, she started to notice everyone's colors. Her fear of doing what she had done the night she saved her mom caused her to stay in and away from the public. Without Caleb to help her, she worried she would do something that could harm his family.

She tried to get the full details from her parents, but if they witnessed her taking a soul, it appeared they were acting passive about it. She recalled her first time seeing Caleb take a soul, she was mortified. She realized how her mom must have felt when she saw what Rayne had done to the man that tried to harm her mom. Rayne thought that might have been why they were acting so reserved about it. She thought that they had already seen her do it once before. None-the-less, they still should have had questions or some sort of curiosity. Rayne still could not understood why they did not question what they witnessed with Rayne's first soul.

Her parent's account of the evening seemed so simple and lacking the most important detail; the soul that saved her life. Janie told Rayne they were seated by a campfire listening to the soft hum of the people that were sitting around the fire with them. She talked about watching the smoke rise from the fire as Rayne was placed next to them on a blanket and the humming got louder. She told Rayne that she and her father listened to lull of the hum and waited as they worked to heal her.

"What did they do to heal me?" Rayne was waiting for her mom to tell her about witnessing a death.

"They just kept humming and Caleb ran away with his sister then the humming got quiet and before we knew it, you were sitting up." Janie smiled as she got to the part about Rayne sitting up.

"That's all?" Rayne could not understand why her mom left out the part where Rayne had to breathe the life out of some stranger. She did not know if her mom was covering up what she had seen, or if she did not know what it was that she was witnessing. She decided to let her mom remember it the way she chose to. "Okay mom, well I feel great now. Whatever they did, it worked. I feel like I can run a marathon."

"You won't be running any marathons today. You need more rest. We were actually minutes away from having the doctor come to the house when Caleb knocked on the door and that's why we ended up with his family." Janie checked Rayne's forehead as she brushed her hair back.

"Don't worry, I said I feel like I could run one. Believe me, I have no intention to actually do it." Rayne smiled at her mom and they both giggled.

Janie started to clean the dishes. There was a knock on the door and Rayne went to answer it while her mom cleaned. It was Caleb. Rayne opened the door and stepped onto the porch. "Hey."

Caleb looked deep into her eyes. "Hey."

Rayne stuttered. "So… thank you."

"I'm glad to see you're up. I thought we lost you for a minute there. How are your parents?" Caleb kept his eyes fixed on Rayne's.

"What do you mean lost me? My mom said I was pretty bad. My parents seem fine. What did they see?" Rayne sounded annoyed as she answered Caleb's questions with more questions.

"You were dying Rayne. Things have changed for you now. I know you don't like it but you have to learn to do this on your own. I thought your parents saw everything. I think something happened and I can't explain it. They didn't say anything?"

"My mom said all she remembers is humming, the smoke from the fire, and you and Selena ran off. The last thing they remember is I was sitting up with them."

"Seriously? Hmm…" Caleb took a minute to go into his own thoughts.

"Caleb what do you mean hmm? What happened to my parents?" Rayne was growing more irritated.

"Nothing happened to your parents. It seemed like they were in a trance. I know it sounds weird but I'm pretty sure that's what happened. I can't imagine that they would be able to comprehend what we have to do to survive. I think my people protected them from witnessing it." Caleb looked confident as he relayed his probable information to Rayne.

Caleb could see discontent with Rayne. He tried to console her. "Not only do we have to do this to survive, we are making life better. We aren't taking anyone who doesn't deserve to be here. I realize we aren't fixing everything, but one by one we make a difference. I have never thought of it any other way, none of us do. We make the world a better place Rayne, you have to believe that or you won't survive. Rayne I need to you… I need you to survive. I'm doing everything I can for you. For your parents."

Rayne could see Caleb was sincere. She almost wanted to hug him but she was still focused on having to kill people. "Caleb, I'm not trying to be difficult. I can see you care, but when you're taught all your life that killing people is bad, it's kind of a hard pill to swallow. I can't just jump into this and you seriously can't expect me to."

"Unfortunately, I do Rayne. You know what just happened to you. You won't survive, this isn't a game." Just as Caleb was pleading, Janie came to the door. She greeted them and asked Caleb if he wanted breakfast. "No thank you ma'am I've had breakfast already. I was just coming by to check on Rayne. She looks healthy."

"I can't thank you enough. I don't know what you and your family did but it was a miracle. Rayne is back to herself." Janie was gushing over Caleb.

"We were glad to help. Honestly we'd feel horrible if anything bad happened to her." Caleb started backing up to leave.

"Thank you." Rayne stepped closer to her mom. Both of them told Caleb bye and went back into the house.

When Janie closed the door she talked about how much she liked Caleb. Rayne did not respond to her. She had wondered if she would like him if she knew what he was and what he did. Rayne could not imagine her mom accepting it, and now Rayne was like Caleb. She felt an empty pain in the pit of her stomach when she thought about it.

Although she was upset and had already eaten, she was able to eat two plates of food. She was piling food into her mouth when she apologized about her voracious eating, then asked a random question. "Sorry I'm eating so much mom. I'm making up for not eating when I was under the weather. So what is it you like about Caleb?" Rayne looked at her plate while she shocked her mom with that question.

Janie looked puzzled by her daughter's question and tried to figure out how to answer it. "Hmm, I'm not sure exactly. There is just something so kind about him. I like that he helped you, that really made your dad and I feel better. I don't know, he's just an easy kid to like. I thought you would be happy with that?"

Rayne was not about to tell her mom that Caleb was the reason she got sick in the first place. She let her mom believe he was who she thought he was. There was no point in approaching the conversation yet. Feeling defeated by her circumstances, depression caused her to spend the day lingering at home. It was early evening when she had given up on the day and went to bed.

Chapter 25

Dream in Unison

Caleb fell asleep by the fire. The dancing smoke and sound of crackles from the sap in the burning pine lulled him to sleep. As he dozed, he was immediately drawn into a dream. It was the night he ran into Rayne. He could clearly see everything as if he were watching a movie. Rayne was walking down the street in the dark and her hands were full with blankets and jackets. She was walking toward a group of men.

Caleb could see the red glow from the men she was headed toward. Only three of the men glowed red. He could barely see Rayne's glow because she was covered with layers of blankets. She had a faint blue radiating from her. As she neared the group of men, he could see that two of them were heading towards her. In his dream state Caleb could feel himself compelled to rush to her rescue.

He could see her nearing the men and suddenly she was slammed to the ground as one of the men with the red glow ran away. Rayne was laying on the street and as her blue glow faded, the other man that glowed was tossed under an oncoming car. Caleb was in the dream now and saw himself lift Rayne and run her to his van. He took her to his family for a day to start her healing. He could recall how he felt the night he rushed her to the hospital. He wanted to pull himself out of the dream. Rayne was the only person he ever helped. She was the only innocent person he ever harmed. When he started to take her soul, a surge rushed through him. In his dream he could sense an energy from Rayne and a power he could not conceive.

He wanted Rayne to live. His sense of regret for harming her was taking over. Her compassion was filling him. The need to love and care for someone, he had never known this feeling before.

He had finally shaken himself awake and attempted to adjust to the reality of how his dream had affected him. He was drenched with perspiration and Selena was staring at him. "Are you okay? What were you dreaming about?" Selena had a husky voice and spoke harshly toward him.

"I'm fine. I didn't dream about anything." Caleb seemed irritated that his sister was watching him and intruding on his personal time and space.

"It sure didn't look like nothing. You were tossing around like a mad man." Now she was chuckling as she spoke.

"You need to stop paying so much attention to me. Get a life." He sounded hostile. He never talked to his sister this way. They were always close. Selena just happened to pick on him at the time he was most vulnerable.

"Whatever!" Selena huffed and walked away.

Caleb remained by the fire and recounted his dream. He also tried to sense what Rayne was thinking. He could feel her relaxed, probably even sleeping.

Rayne was sleeping. She had been asleep for a few hours before the dream came over her. It was the same one Caleb had although she had no idea he dreamt it. She was seeing it the same way he did, from a spectator's perspective. She could see herself walking toward the men. She could see their red glow. Being able to see like this was new to her. Seeing people in color, seeing them for who they were. She could now see that the men she was walking toward were bad.

As she watched, she could sense that the person she was watching had a faint blue glow and was heading toward trouble. That was when she noticed she was that girl heading toward trouble. The group of men she was about to help intended on harming her, then suddenly she was slammed to the ground. She could see Caleb scoop her up and run her to the van. At that point in her dream she started to feel tired and fell off into a deep sleep until morning.

When she woke up, she was rested. After she wiped the sleep from her eyes, she started to remember her dream. She remembered it completely. She realized that somehow she needed the dream. It was as if it came to her on purpose and gave her answers she needed. Caleb saved her that night. She might be different now, but she was here. She was grateful and ashamed at the same time. Ashamed because until her dream, she had been angry. Angry with Caleb for what he had done to her. Now she knew the truth, what he had done for her was saved her. He was the one who knocked her to the ground but if he were not there to take a soul, Rayne would not be alive to dream anymore.

Rayne leapt out of bed. She rushed to get dressed and ran to get a breakfast bar then kissed her parents cheeks as she whirled through the kitchen. They stared at her as she blurted out that she was in a hurry to go see Caleb. They were happy she was better and Caleb was the reason, they did not contest her going. They asked her to be careful and to call if she was going to be too long.

She drove up to where she would have to park and make her way by foot through the forest to get to his camp. She ran through the trees and as she was rounding a corner that was obstructed by trees she slammed into Caleb. They did not hit hard enough to get hurt but Caleb wrapped his arms around her and asked if she was ok. She shook her head and just stared at him and pulled his arms off of her. "What's wrong? Why are you here?" Rayne still stared at him while he spoke. "Rayne, are you okay?"

She finally spoke. "Thank you." Her cheeks were pink and her eyes were glassy. Caleb could not help but think how beautiful she was.

"For what?" He brushed the hair from her forehead.

"You saved me. I saw it. Last night I had a dream. It was the night I was in the accident. It was you. You took me to the hospital. You saved me from those men. You saved me this weekend. You saved me for my parents."

"Wait, you had the dream too?" Caleb held her by her shoulders and studied her face.

"Yeah, the one from the night of the accident."

"Rayne, I'm sorry. I didn't mean to hurt you. I didn't mean to turn you into this." He was still holding her when he spoke.

"Don't worry. I understand now. You had no other choice. You had the dream too. You saw those men. You know what they were going to do. I'm here talking to you because you were there to protect me. No matter what I am now, I'm happy to be here." She leaned in toward him and hugged him.

He smiled has she hugged him. The smell of her hair and the warmth of her embrace stirred strong unfamiliar emotions in him. He was happy she was the one to take the initiative to bring them closer. In his culture there was no need for an embrace. He was compelled to wrap his arms around her. The two stayed locked together for a few minutes before Caleb took her by the hand and they walked to camp.

Caleb had become highly respected among his family and as they walked through, each family member they passed smiled at them. It was an unusual sight for Caleb. By the time they sat with Selena, she was laughing. "Look at you two, the cute couple." That was when Caleb realized he was still holding Rayne's hand. He pulled his hand away.

"Shut up." Caleb looked sternly at his sister. She was older than him but he had taken on more authority than her.

"Sorry brother." She smiled and nodded her head toward her family, "They've been humming about you two all morning. There's so much chatter I can't get them out of my head."

"I know, I feel it too. I can't think straight." Caleb sat and Rayne sat next to him. Rayne felt the same sense of confusion but she did not say anything. Caleb looked at her as she stayed thinking silently. It looked as if he knew what she was thinking and she blushed when he smiled at her.

Selena was the one person Caleb confided in. They were brought to the family at the same time and they grew up together. Although they had no genetic bond, they looked like each other.

"So what was your dream? It must be something major because it's making everyone crazy here." Selena was talking low, knowing that no matter how quietly she spoke, they all could hear her.

"Rayne and I both had the same dream. That's why she's here." Rayne stayed quiet while Caleb spoke.

"So are you gonna tell me about this dream or do I have to try to have the dream too?" Selena chuckled as she nodded in Rayne's direction.

Rayne looked at Caleb wondering if she was supposed to tell his sister the dream. Caleb nodded his head and Rayne proceeded to tell her story. When she was done, Selena sat silent for a moment then spoke up. "Do we need to go to Superior about this?"

"I don't think so. Not yet. It seems like things are going how they are supposed to. I think the family knows this. I'm going to wait a week." Caleb got up and pulled Rayne to her feet. "We need to go. You need to get home. I don't want your parents worrying about you anymore."

"Bye, Selena." Rayne spoke quietly as she waved.

When they got to the car Caleb talked a bit more. "You graduate next week right?" Rayne shook her head yes. "Okay, have your parents said anything? Are they acting different?"

"Well my mom has decided she likes you. As a matter of fact she made it a point to emphasize it." She gave him a puzzling smile.

"Strange I guess." Caleb had the same puzzled look. "Well that's better than her not liking me." They both laughed. Something about Rayne had changed him. It was harder to let her go every time he had to leave her.

Chapter 26

Graduation

The week passed leaving one more until graduation. There were senior festivities as all

the kids were preparing to move onto adulthood. Rayne did not share the same

enthusiasm as her class-men. She had a new motivation and it was not college. Rayne

was curious about Caleb and his family. She had inadvertently become one of them but

was still an outsider. Slowly she was being incorporated with them but the apprehension

was felt by both families.

Although Rayne's parents liked Caleb, they did not like that Rayne had lost focus on

college and her future. The conversation came up every morning at breakfast. Rayne's

dad was trying to find a middle ground and insistently brought up community college.

Rayne tried to convince her dad that she would only take a year off and work.

As graduation grew closer, Rayne noticed she was getting weaker and could see everyone

around her shining brighter every day. She was learning that it meant it was time for her

to visit Caleb's family.

Rayne held out as long as she could, but the day before graduation Caleb came to her

house. "You need to come now. Haven't you learned how important it is? You're going to get sick again." While they were sitting on the porch talking, Janie came and told

Caleb hello. She asked him if he would be coming to the graduation and he told her that

both he and his sister would be attending. Rayne told her mom that she was going to visit

his family but she would be home by 9:00. Janie let her go because she did not have to

wake up early the next morning. Her mom reminded her that, although she was eighteen,

she still lived at home and had to follow the rules at home. "I will mom, don't worry. I'm

not about to become 'that kid'." She gave her mom a hug before she left with Caleb.

Because hunting was a new skill Rayne had to learn, Caleb wanted to make sure the sun

was down before they hunted. The hunting party consisted of Rayne, Caleb, and Selena.

Caleb and Selena usually went together so they could watch out for each other.

Unfortunately, there was an abundance of dark souls that moved through the area. It was

why the family chose to settle there. With a constant flow of traffic and the degenerates

that inhabit that portion of the town, they could live there undetected for a long time.

When Rayne took her first soul, she acted upon instinct and survival for her parents. She

could see the man that was about to hurt her mother was dark and his aura was bright red

and black. He had no regard for her life or the life of others. Her second soul, the

perverted teacher, was a simple kill and easier to cover up. Now that she was hunting

with Caleb and Selena, she was nervous. Caleb and his sister could sense it. They both

comforted her and told her it will come natural. Rayne doubted them as she followed.

They went to an area in town that was known for its ill behavior. The three sat in an ally and waited. It smelt foul and Rayne was ready to leave. Within a minute of her thought, her senses were heightened. That was when Caleb and Selena seemed to have disappeared. The ally was dark and Rayne could see a figure walking toward her. She did not know if it was a man or woman, she could only see the red glow around the large figure that was moving slowly.

Rayne felt her anger grow. His soul was fiercely dark. She fought the urge to pounce. He got closer and spoke, "Hey honey, you shouldn't be out here alone. Let me help you." He was a foot away from her when he reached out for her. She leapt on him and knocked him down. There was barely a struggle when she inhaled his life. He was placed on the pungent ground, alongside of the building. Rayne did not have to adjust him or hide him.

She sat up and looked around noticing Caleb and Selena right next to her. "Where did you go?"

"We were right here. You did well." Caleb put his hand out to help Rayne up.

They left the ally and walked back toward their camp. Rayne noticed Caleb walking a little slower. "Is everything okay?"

"Yeah." Caleb seemed winded in his response.

They were heading toward an encampment and Selena tugged Rayne to walk with her while Caleb pulled back a bit. As they walked Rayne asked Selena if her brother was safe walking alone. "Yeah, he'll be fine."

Rayne heard talking. It sounded like drunk chatter. They were getting closer to a group of loud men. There was a time when this would make Rayne uncomfortable but with her new skills she had the confidence of an army. They walked past where all the ruckus was coming from when she heard one of the men walking behind them. He sounded belligerent and vulgar. He was getting closer when suddenly Rayne heard a thud. It sounded like a body hitting the ground, a sound she was becoming familiar with.

Caleb had taken the man. He pulled him to the trees when he was done then caught up with the girls. Rayne realized this was how they hunted. As Selena lured the men out with her beauty, it was a guarantee that she would intrigue the darkest of humans. Selena was beautiful, so using her as bait was an obvious beneficial tactic.

It was 8:30 at night and they still had to get back to Caleb's van. Feeling full of energy, the three ran back to camp. Before Rayne climbed into the passenger seat, Selena stopped her, "I know I shouldn't be surprised, but you did very well tonight." She smiled at her.

Rayne smiled back. "Thank you." Rayne knew that Selena was offering a genuine compliment.

They barely got to the front door before 9:00. There was not enough time for a proper goodbye. Rayne told Caleb she would see him tomorrow for her graduation. Rayne popped her head into her parent's room and told them good night before she went to sleep.

They woke up early the next morning and Janie made a big breakfast for the three. Mornings were Janie's favorite time of day. More often than not, it was the one time of day they were together. They all talked about graduation and the topic of college surfaced. Rayne asked her dad if she could work for him or try to work at the school district with her mom. Her dad did not oppose the idea and said they would talk about it later.

Caleb and Selena were waiting at the school entrance when Rayne arrived. Caleb was anxious to see Rayne. He never knew anticipation like this before. Selena hugged Rayne first. Rayne was shocked by her gesture of kindness. After Selena was done, Caleb stepped up for his turn. When Caleb put his arms around her, her heart pulsed and it felt like butterflies were dancing under her skin. They smiled at each other as the crowd broke their embrace.

Everyone went to their seats while Rayne took her place in the commencement line up. As Rayne stood with her classmates, she reflected on her year. She was standing there about to graduate, when many months ago she was broken and in the hospital. The thought brought a smile to her face. Knowing Caleb sat in the audience watching her made her smile beam.

The ceremony was long but entertaining and filled with speeches, as well as a surprise tribute to Rayne. She received an award for accomplishing graduation after her trying ordeal.

Once graduation was over, they all went to dinner to celebrate. The evening was perfect. After dinner, Caleb asked if Rayne could come visit with them. Rayne's parents allowed her to go but reminded her of her curfew.

They all parted and Rayne went to Caleb's camp while her parents went home. As Tom walked toward the front door he noticed a card wedged in the crack of the door. It was from the sheriff that responded to the incident the night that Janie was nearly attacked. There was a note scribbled on the back telling him to call as soon as possible.

He called when he got in the house but was directed to the sheriff's voicemail. After Tom left the message he tried to figure out what the officer wanted. He talked with Janie about it but the two came up with nothing. It did however, remind them of that night. They had gotten over what they witnessed but they had not forgotten. It was unexplainable and the couple chose to avoid it completely.

Rayne was happy to be visiting with Caleb's family. She found that, more and more, she was drawn to commune with them. While they were all sitting around the fire Caleb told Rayne that they would be taking a summer trip to Arizona in order to visit the rest of their family. He asked if she would be interested in going and if she thought her parents would allow her to go.

As much as she wanted to go, Rayne was not sure. She never spent time away from them and going off with Caleb might not be a good place to start. "Maybe I could tell them Selena asked if I could go with her. I'd hate to lie, but I'm guessing they wouldn't be too happy if I asked if I could go with you."

Caleb agreed and told her when they planned on going so she could tell her parents. They would only be gone for a week. Rayne told him she would try but no promises.

Chapter 27

Disturbing Call

The next morning the sheriff returned Tom's call. He asked Tom if he could remember

the evening of the attack in good detail. Tom was curious about what the sheriff was

inquiring for. The report should have had everything he needed in order to close the case.

The sheriff informed him that during the autopsy, it looked as if the perpetrator had some

type of injury to his esophagus. It was a strange injury that could not be explained by

natural causes.

Tom told the sheriff that he did not witness anything odd. The report that the family gave

the sheriff was that during the attack Rayne walked up and shoved the man that away

from her mother. As she pushed him he appeared to grab his chest and he fell to the

ground. When he stayed down for a few minutes Tom checked his pulse and that was

when they called the police and ambulance. He said he had no idea what could have

happened to his throat.

The sheriff thanked him for his time and that if he had any more questions he would call

back. Tom told him he was more than happy helping. After he hung up, he called home.

Janie answered and he told her what happened then he asked to talk to Rayne. Tom told her that he needed to talk to her when he got home so she needed to be there. Rayne promised she would stay.

When Tom got home they discussed what had happened the night of the accident. Tom asked Rayne if she remembered what happened. Rayne got nervous. She did not know what to tell her dad. She remembered in detail what happened and that the result was the safety of her family.

Her dad tried to stay calm and think of different ways to approach his questioning. The only outcome of everything he asked was the same answer "I remember knocking him down, that's all." She made sure to keep her voice steady when she spoke. Tom asked her "You don't remember getting in his face when he was on the ground?"

"No I don't. Why would I do that?" She kept her composure as she responded.

"I don't know. I thought it was strange too. What I do know is whatever you did saved us but killed him." Tom did not want to sound accusatory toward his daughter.

"I thought it was a heart attack that killed him, or drugs or something."

"The sheriff called me today and told me that something happened to his throat. It wasn't a natural injury. The sheriff wanted to know if we knew anything about it."

"I don't know, dad. Nothing happened to his throat when I pushed him. Maybe it happened before he attacked us but it wasn't from me." Rayne wanted the conversation to end, she hated lying to her father. Just then Janie walked in and defused the tension. Their talk transitioned to when Rayne planned on starting work. That was when she took the opportunity to ask about going to Arizona with Selena. It would be a short trip and a nice little vacation for her before she started work.

Her parents told her that she was eighteen and could make decisions on her own as long as she was responsible about her choices. They would allow her to go but she had to be serious about work when she got back. Rayne told them she would and thanked them both with a hug.

Chapter 28

Travel

Rayne was packed and ready to leave. She had breakfast with her parents before her dad left for work. She was hoping he would be gone before Caleb came to pick her up. She did not mention his name when she asked permission to go. She masked it by saying she would be traveling with Selena and her family, that way she would not be lying.

Tom drove off and Caleb pulled up. Janie greeted him when he came to the door to get Rayne's bags. Selena stood with him and smiled at Janie while the two chatted. Janie reminded Rayne to keep her phone charged and stay in contact so they would not worry. Rayne gave her mom a hug and piled into the van with her friends.

Rayne had not left town for the past few years and was excited as they drove off. This trip was a much needed getaway for her. The weather was good and they arrived to the mountains in Arizona within the day.

The camp was peaceful as they pulled in. There were saguaro cactus and indigenous foliage covering the landscape. The clean smell of desert mountains tickled Rayne's nose. She could not imagine why Caleb and his family chose not to live there.

They were greeted when they walked into camp. Two older women took Rayne by the arm while Caleb and Selena followed behind. Rayne looked back at Caleb with concern. She had no idea what was happening but she had heard Caleb's voice in her head telling her everything would be fine. She was led to the fire and placed in front of an older man. He looked strong and tall, Rayne thought he might be Polynesian. He stood and took her by her shoulders. She could hear a different voice in her head. "My child, I'm so pleased to meet you. You have great strength." Rayne blushed feeling the depth of his compliment. She did not know this man, but she knew he was important.

Caleb and Selena were both in awe when they watched as Superior put his arms around Rayne in an embrace. It was uncharacteristic of anyone in their family to show outward affection. After he released his hold, he placed Rayne next to him and they all sat. She could hear him in her head again. "You have much to learn in a short time. You have the strength to learn." The fire crackled as she listened to his voice.

Everyone remained quiet while they sat. Dinner was brought to them and they ate silently. Finally as they finished their last bites the Superior spoke. "Rayne needs our guidance. She is here not by chance but by providence and her accident with Caleb was part of the process to bring her position to fruition. We are blessed to have her and she must be treated as the blessing she is." His face was solemn as he spoke. Caleb was surprised as he listened.

Rayne thought to Caleb and he could hear her. "Caleb I don't know what is happening."

Caleb responded "I don't either." Just then they both heard Superior's voice, "You two will learn soon enough."

After his speech, he requested the two women to bring dessert. The women seemed pleased to serve everyone. Rayne tried to imagine these sweet old women taking souls. She enjoyed the stone oven baked pastry. After they were done eating, Rayne was taken to her sleeping tent. There was a wash basin and an ornately decorated cot. She was smitten with the quaint dimly lit space.

She cleaned up for bed and called her mom before she went to sleep. She apologized for not calling when they arrived then she boasted about her tent and the good food. Janie was happy to hear her daughter was enjoying herself.

Rayne slept peacefully through the night. In the morning, Selena came into her tent to wake her up. They were going on a hike and wanted to start before the sun came up. Selena told Rayne that she did not want to miss the sunrise. She boasted that it would be like no other.

Caleb, Rayne, and Selena were handed a leather bag full of food before they set off. As they started on their path, they were accompanied by a pack of coyotes. They ascended up the steepest mountain. The coyotes led the way. The three where quiet as they walked. They had finally reached a plateau and sat on a hollow log, then watched as the sunrise broke the horizon. It was more breathtaking than Rayne had imagined. While they watched, Caleb placed his hand on top of Rayne's. Her heart pulsed so intensely, she felt as if she was feeling his heart beat. She did not break her gaze from the vibrant skyline.

Selena spoke but also kept her eyes fixed on the view, "Superior says this is as close to Heaven on earth that we can get. It's beautiful isn't it?" She was thinking out loud not expecting a response when Caleb spoke. "Beautiful, yes." He was talking about both Rayne and the view.

The sun was nearly full when they decided to eat then head back down the hill. Rayne could not believe how amazing the food tasted. Unsure if it was because of how it was prepared or the ambiance, she could not get enough of the culinary explosion she was enjoying. She glanced at Caleb as she shoved another piece of bread in her mouth. He smiled at her and again she was blushing. "I'm glad you like it" he said as she tried to swallow it down and respond. "It's amazing!" Rayne was unable to contain her enthusiasm for her meal. Selena and Caleb both laughed.

Laughter was once a sarcastic noise they would make but with Rayne it was genuine pleasure. She brought out a happiness in them. It was a unique experience for the two. Caleb thought to himself, this must be what the Superior meant when he said Rayne was a blessing.

Caleb helped Rayne to her feet and they all started their decent back down to camp. They were quiet when they walked. The sounds around them were too delightful to stifle with conversation.

They spent the rest of their days hiking and enjoying the company of the tribe. The entire time, they did not realize they were being watched and guided by their leader. He was pleased with the relationship the three shared.

After they were packed and ready to head home, Superior hugged all of them individually and put a different thought in each of their head but requested that they keep it to themselves. His thought for Rayne was to learn to accept her life and adjust approaching her prey with appreciation rather than hate and anger. He let her know that because she is a rare blessing, she has to work harder to adjust than the children that are born into the life. He gave Caleb the suggestion to start accepting and reciprocating what Rayne had to share. Also to be open to the new pleasures and sensations, but always be diligent to his path. Finally, he tasked Selena to understand the new changes she would be witnessing in her brother. Selena was to be the confidant that both Caleb and Rayne would need.

Their drive home was peaceful and uneventful. Rayne made sure to keep her mom current on their location so she would not worry. Once they arrived in town, they dropped Rayne off and gave her a hug before they drove away. Caleb did not want to leave her and Rayne did not want to leave them but she missed her parents and were happy to see them.

Rayne spent the rest of the day telling her parents about what she had experienced. She told about the unique way Selena and Caleb's family lived, and how beautiful the whole trip was.

Chapter 29

Reality

They were barely back a full day before Rayne noticed she was getting tired easily. It was a feeling she was starting to recognize and tried not to dread. She was going to have to go see Caleb as soon as she got up in the morning.

Through the night she tossed around while she dreamt about the last time she took a soul. Although she knew it was just a dream, she could sense Caleb reassuring her that he was there for her.

The next morning when she woke, Caleb was knocking at her door. Rayne's parents were at work and the knock was constant. As she was trying to get to the door, Caleb opened it and pushed his way in. He knew Rayne was weak but they could not go until dusk. He had helped her call her parents to let them know that she was going to spend the day with his family. Her dad needed to be convinced and reminded her that she would be working soon, but her mom was happy to let her go.

She struggled to get dressed and Caleb waited outside of her bedroom door in case she fell. Before they left she grabbed some breakfast bars. He had to help her climb into the seat of his van. She was able to buckle herself in as they sped off.

Although it was daylight, the fire was crackling when they arrived to the camp. Caleb carried Rayne from where he was parked to her spot around the fire. The whole scene was routine. The hum of the family, the smell of the fire and the crows in the trees.

They patiently awaited dusk. When the time was right, Caleb and his sister helped to carry Rayne. They knew she had to start doing it on her own. Until she did, they needed to support her. They found a location near a hidden biker bar. It was easy to find what they needed at the bar but the risk was the greater. There rarely was a lone wolf among the biker community, especially this crowd. These bad guys traveled in packs and dealing with them was always too risky for the family. This time, the risk outweighed the consequence. For Rayne, not getting a soul was akin to dying of thirst, and this time it was coming on quickly.

They moved swiftly through the tree line in the direction of the noisy crowd. They were hoping that one of the guys would wonder off to relieve himself. They sat quietly in the area that wreaked of urine. Rayne was too weak to notice the foul smell.

Within the hour they saw someone coming. The glow was bright red and Rayne felt a pulse of energy. Before Caleb and Selena could react Rayne pounced on a large man covered in tattoos. He was knocked to the ground and dead in less than thirty seconds. Suddenly there was the sound of a crowd heading towards them and they had to pull Rayne up quickly to leave.

A small angry crowd started to chase them through the trees. Rayne had her energy back and could keep up with Caleb and Selena. It was dark as they dashed through the forest. They managed to run fast enough to create a big gap between the men when suddenly, there were gunshots. The three ran without looking back. They could not go back to their camp with the crowd following them so they ran in a different direction. Caleb made sure to communicate with them through thoughts. There were coyotes running with them now and Caleb directed some of them to go back to the family to warn them.

The sound of gunshots were far away now, but Rayne panicked when she heard the ricochet of a stray bullet whiz past her ear. Caleb stayed inside her thoughts, reassuring her that they would be fine. Finally, they were far enough away that they could slow down and look back. Caleb could faintly see two people that glowed red. He decided that it would be a good idea to sit and wait to see if they would come closer. He and Selena needed a soul and considering their predicament, it was a good opportunity.

They could not hear anyone. There were only crackling leaves and snapping twigs in the far off distance but the crackling sound was heading their way. Caleb could see the glow coming closer. He told Rayne to stay in her position while he and Selena took care of the two. Three minutes passed and the people were right on them. Selena and Caleb remained calm as they stood still behind a pair of thick tree trunks.

Rayne was nervous and antsy. She squeezed her hands into tight fists. The two people that were out to kill them were feet away from the trees that Caleb and Selena were behind. In one synchronized motion, both soul stealers took down their aggressors. Rayne was shocked to see one of them was a woman. She shivered when she saw Caleb lift himself from the female stranger. "Yes Rayne, women are bad too. We don't see their gender, we see their darkness." Caleb said it out loud because he could hear what Rayne was thinking.

They left the bodies and ran back toward the direction parallel to their camp. Once they were sure they were not being followed, they walked back into their camp. The family was grateful to see them. They were concerned that they would not make it back alive. The three rested by the fire before they drove Rayne back home. Rayne was relieved to be back and at the same time she felt invigorated by the attack. Her energy was back and her angst for taking another life was diminishing.

They had settled and got their breath back before it was time to take Rayne home. She did not want to leave but she knew her parents would worry. More and more, Caleb's family started to feel like her family. She felt distant when she was away from them, from the circle.

When Caleb walked her to the door he hesitated to walk away. He was fighting the urge to hug her. He was drawn to her. He wanted to touch her, smell her hair. He wanted to kiss her. He never kissed anyone, ever. Just as he moved in toward her, Janie opened the front door. "Hi you two. I was starting to get worried. I hope you had a good day. Your dad is asking when you're going to go into his office so today may be your last day of freedom." Janie gave a wink when she finished the sentence and backed into the house.

"I'll go in with him tomorrow mom. Goodnight Caleb." Rayne turned to walk in the door. She did not want Caleb to leave but she knew her mom was going to come back out and hover until she was back inside.

"Rayne I'm sorry about tonight. I never meant to put you in a situation like that. I never want to think about hurting you." Caleb took her hand as he spoke.

"Caleb you were trying to help me. We could have never guessed that would happen. We made it out okay." She smiled at him as she spoke. She was smiling because she was excited that he took her hand. Her palm started to sweat as she thought of the simple pleasure of holding his hand. Their touch felt like electricity, like a current connecting each other.

"That doesn't make it okay. I don't know what I would do if something happened to you." His head was lowered when he said this and he gazed at her in an intense angle. Their thoughts were twisted within each other. They could not hear what was in their minds, and it seemed their thoughts for one another were stuck in a strange gridlock.

Janie popped her head out again. "It's getting late and you need to get ready for tomorrow, plus dinner is getting cold."

"Sorry mom. I'll be right in." She turned to tell Caleb goodbye. She did not want to let go of his hand.

"Can I see you tomorrow after you're done with your dad?" He was squeezing her hand softly. He had to force himself to let go of her.

"Of course. You'll come get me?" Rayne was hoping he would say yes.

"I'll be here at 5:30." He smiled when he let go of her hand.

"See you then." She turned and went inside.

Chapter 30

Fallen Officer

Rayne woke up when her parents did. They all ate breakfast together. She was not in a

rush to go to work with her dad, but she was anxious to get the day done so she could see

Caleb.

Tom's office was small. He shared it with his partner. They were family law attorneys

but on occasion they would do some defense work. Rayne had been there many times

before, but this was the first time she would be working.

The drive was quiet. Tom listened to talk radio, and Rayne had her headphones on. The

office was twenty-five minutes away if there was no traffic. They pulled into a parking

spot and Rayne helped carry her dad's files and computer into the office. Tom picked up

the newspaper on the way in.

Inside, Tom started to read the paper after he set up a space for Rayne. The headline story

was about a local police officer and lawyer dying in the forest along the Ortega Highway.

Tom recognized the lawyer's name. She was a defense attorney with a history of

unscrupulous clients and behavior. He did not recognize the police officer's name and there was another person who had died as well, but the name was not being released until the person's next of kin was notified.

Tom did not mention anything to Rayne because it was not something she would have been interested in. They went about their day at the office and Rayne did the filing and answered the phone for him.

After they got home, the topic of conversation at dinner was the story Tom had read earlier. Janie and Tom did not notice when Rayne quietly gasped. Janie asked about the lawyer. She thought she recalled the name in a conversation she and Tom had in the past.

"Yeah, that's her. Her clients are connected and she dabbles in human trafficking or at least she defends those that find it an acceptable form of revenue. The paper said they were doing an autopsy because of the whole scene. It looks like they all died from natural causes but according to witnesses they were chasing some people that were hiding in the woods." Tom seemed disgusted as he spoke. It was obvious he did not care for the woman and probably did not feel bad for her passing.

"Well it sounds like the world won't be missing someone like that. I know it sounds horrible to say, but it sounds like she was repulsive and it's probably better that she's gone." Janie took a bite as soon as she finished her thought.

Rayne did not share in the conversation. She kept her face toward her plate and thoughts to herself.

Just as the dinner dishes were cleaned, Caleb knocked on the door. Rayne excused herself from her parents and went for a walk with Caleb. During the walk, she told him about the news. He was not shocked because he had never cared about the people he took. He was not born to care, he was born to cure the world of despicable behavior. He told her not to worry. She could not help but worry since they had nearly been caught and shot when the whole thing went down. Again, Caleb could hear her concern as she thought and reassured her that he would not let anything happen to her.

He desperately wanted to put his arm around her as they walked, but he was not sure how she would respond, so he just walked close to her. He was frustrated that he could not sense how she felt about him. He could hear almost all of her thoughts when he needed to. When it came to trying to hear how she felt about him, things seemed confusing and crossed.

Rayne was wishing he would hold her hand. She loved walking next to him. She thought that the gift of being inside one another's head would help her to know what he thought of, her but all she got was jumbled sound. Her only conclusion was that he was not interested in her. She wished she could hear what was inside his head when he was not thinking of hunting.

He walked her back home and hesitated when they got to her porch. It was nearly painful keeping his distance from her. "I'll come back tomorrow if that's okay?" He knew he had to leave before he tried to touch her. He had hugged her before but not in an intimate situation like this. He had to get away from her.

"Okay. Same time?" She wished he would hug her again.

"Sure." He turned and walked away.

Rayne went inside feeling disappointed. Her parents were watching the news. It was more of the story about what happened in the woods at Ortega. The third person was finally named and was deemed a career criminal. He had been on trial numerous times for drugs, money laundering, human trafficking and offenses against children. He was also named as a constant client for the lawyer that had died. The news reported their deaths as mysterious. Rayne thought to herself that they did not know the half of it. Knowing more about the souls she was collecting, put her at ease about taking them.

She went to bed so she could be up early to go with her dad to work. The next morning the routine was the same. A quiet drive, her dad picked up the paper, and they went into the office. Rayne wanted to talk to her dad about the accident. "Dad, what do you think about that lawyer and cop that died? Do you feel the same way as mom?"

"I don't know Rayne. It's hard for me to say considering I'm a lawyer. I do believe in the justice system but sometimes when casualties like this happen, it works more justly than the legal system. Personally, I think these people are scum. I've never liked the clientele she represented and I'm pretty sure that cop that died with her may have been a partner of hers. I've heard of him and as I recall, he's been caught with his hands in hot water. I'm sure he was a client of hers more than once."

"I guess I kind of agree as well. Do you think they'll find out what happened to them? I mean it's strange and random that all three of them would die of natural causes at the same time in the same area." Rayne was trying to feel her father out.

"Yeah it's strange, but I don't care. They're gone." He was done with the conversation.

Rayne was content with his response and went on with her work. They finished out their day and went home. At dinner Rayne scarfed her food so she could be ready when Caleb came. She waited but he never came.

The rest of the week passed the same way, and Caleb never came. Rayne was confused. She missed him and did not know why he was staying away. She could not hear his thoughts of comfort that he usually sent when she worried.

Chapter 31

Mysterious Autopsy

The week passed and the autopsies were completed on the three people found dead in the woods. They all had crushed esophagi and lung damage. There were no markings on the exterior part of their necks, the damage was completely internal. The coroner had never seen anything like it. He looked in the records for the previous coroner and there were two other cases similar, both deemed natural causes of death but with extenuating circumstances. Collapsed esophagus would be named the circumstances.

One of the two named in the recorded autopsies was the man Rayne took when she was protecting her parents. After his records were found, his history surfaced. The man had many charges against him and served in prison for manslaughter. He was listed on the pedophile list and was not allowed to live within a quarter of a mile from schools because of his lewd acts with children. The man was a foul degenerate. Rayne knew that when she took his soul.

After the findings, an officer visited Tom again. He discussed what was found and asked Tom if he was sure that they did not see anything else. Tom reassured him that they had given the whole story. The officer asked Tom to keep an eye on Rayne and note if she started developing any illnesses in case she had contracted something from the man that attacked them. After he said goodbye to the officer, he reflected on the events of that night.

He remembered Rayne taking the man down. He was not sure what she was doing or how she wrestled with him like she had, but he did not see her put her hands around the man's neck. Tom really thought the man had a heart attack or died from some kind of drug overdose.

Tom asked Rayne if there was something he missed in the attack but she told him it was as they reported to the police. All she did was knock him down. That was exactly the way Tom saw it as well.

Rayne still had not heard from Caleb, and with the new information about the related injuries of the victims, she started to worry more. She could not concentrate or eat. It was not time for her to find a soul but the anxiety was getting to her. She missed Caleb and needed him.

As she was settling into a sadness from missing Caleb, there was a knock at the front door. It was Caleb. Rayne wanted to jump into his arms when she opened the door. She stayed standing in the doorway acting cool and distant. "Hey."

Caleb hesitated before he spoke. "I'm sorry I stayed away."

Rayne wanted to burst into tears. The stress from the week and not seeing Caleb had worn on her. Prideful, she chose to stay cool. "It's ok. I'm sure you had your reasons." Caleb did not understand why she was acting like this. He knew she had a lot on her mind. He had wanted to come earlier for many reasons. He needed to help her, but selfishly he wanted to be near her. "It's not okay. I really am sorry. There was no reason. I thought you needed some space. I'm so confused with you Rayne. I can tell you're upset. Your thoughts are all so cluttered and wild. I can't figure this out and I don't know what to do."

When he reminded her he could hear her thoughts, she defended her concerns. "I'm just worried about those last people we took. I don't think this is going to disappear so easily." She was telling part of what was cluttered in her head. The rest of the clutter was how she felt about Caleb.

"Rayne I don't know how to say this. We have to leave. Things aren't safe anymore and you are right to be worried. Friends of those people we took are looking for us now. We will be leaving before the weekend." He did not look up at her when he spoke.

"Where will you go?" Rayne was crushed. She did not want him to go. She did not know what she would do without him or his family.

"Rayne you don't understand. You need to come with us. You won't survive without us." Now Caleb was looking right into her eyes.

There was a long silence. Rayne did not know what to think. She now had to choose between Caleb and her parents. She was old enough to leave but she had not intended on leaving her parents so soon.

Caleb knew what she was thinking now. He understood her concern about leaving her parents. He understood because he felt the same about leaving her. "We'll be going to Arizona for a while. We intend to come back here but we'll have to see how everything goes." Caleb had hoped that telling her this would help to convince her to join him.

"Caleb do you really think my parents will let me go?"

"Rayne you're 18. You can leave on your own."

"It's just not that easy. It's not the way things work with my parents."

"Tell them you're going to college there. My family will pay your tuition. You won't be lying. Rayne it's important, if you stay here your parents won't have a daughter to send to college." Caleb was trying to sell her on this move and it was working.

"Let me talk to them. Come back tomorrow."

"I will." Caleb had a look of sincerity.

"No seriously come back this time, I mean it. You can't leave me like that again." She kept her hands crossed so she would not reach out for him. She liked his half smile, it was reassuring.

Her plea to see him again was a good sign to Caleb. He had hoped it meant she was serious about going away with him. "I promise, I'll be back. Now start working on your parents."

"Okay, see you tomorrow." She went inside before goodbye became more difficult.

While she waited for dinner, Rayne jumped on her laptop to check out Arizona State University. There was a good four year program for business and agriculture. Both were things she had always been interested in. She checked on the community college as well in case she missed the fall registration cutoff.

At dinner she waited for the perfect time to start the discussion for the move. First everyone talked more about the dead lawyer then Rayne hit them with the topic of college.

"Dad I've been thinking more about college lately. I've checked out Arizona State and they have two degrees I'm interested. I started my paperwork for registration, I hope you're okay with that." Rayne decided it was better to ask forgiveness than permission in the situation.

"Why do you want to go all the way to Arizona? Isn't it too late to start in the fall?" Tom was caught off guard by his daughter's request.

"I have another week to fill out the forms plus I checked out the community college up there just in case. Caleb's family will help me out. I won't be alone." Rayne tried to be as convincing as possible. It was working, or so she thought.

"You're not doing this just because of Caleb are you? I don't want you chasing a boy, I want you chasing your dreams." Tom peered at her under his eyebrows.

"No dad, I'm not. Besides, things are getting strange here. There's so much violence. It's peaceful in Arizona and beautiful in the mountains. I fell in love with it when I went out there. Seriously, I'm not chasing after Caleb. Do you really think it's like me to do that?" Actually that's exactly what she was doing. She was going because Caleb needed her to go and she wanted to be with him. Going to college was a bonus.

"What's the tuition and where will you be living?"

"I could stay with Caleb and Selena's family so I can save money there and I don't know the tuition yet, but Caleb said his family would help pay if we needed them to." Rayne knew she had to be careful or she would sound like she was going for him.

"And you're sure you're not going just because of him?" Tom set his fork down.

"I'm sure dad. I love it there and the opportunity is perfect." Rayne took a bite so she would look less desperate.

"Show me what you come up with and we'll discuss it on the way to the office." Tom finished his dinner.

Rayne was happy. She knew that her dad had already made up his mind but the formality of talking about it had to be covered in order to complete the deal. She helped her mom with the dishes and went to bed.

In the morning, she gave her dad the amounts for tuition and the programs she was looking into. She also gave him the info on the community college so that he would know she was serious about school. He half-heartedly said yes and as he was picking up the newspaper she gave him a hug.

Chapter 32

The Move Postponed

Caleb came over when he said he would. Rayne told him that her dad was apprehensive but decided to let her go and that she had to be serious about school. Caleb was excited with the news and wanted to take Rayne away right then. It took all of his strength to keep from grabbing her and wrapping her in his arms.

Just as that thought nearly took him over, the door opened. It was Tom. "We need to talk Caleb." He turned to walk away and motioned Caleb to follow him.

Inside he motioned Caleb to sit on the couch. "Rayne will be safe with my family Sir." Caleb sensed what was on Tom's mind.

"You understand my worries. I don't know what your intentions are with Rayne, but I think her education needs to come before anything else." Tom was stern when he spoke.

Caleb never had to have a conversation convincing a father to let his daughter leave with him. He approached it with complete honesty. His only intention was to keep Rayne safe. "I have no intentions besides keeping her safe. She will be going to school and she will have her own living space. I can assure you, she will be safe."

They finished their conversation, but Tom already knew that Rayne had made up her mind to leave. He had to learn accept it. "When will you be leaving?"

Caleb did not hesitate "We will be leaving this week Sir. My family is packing now."

"This week? That isn't much notice." Tom did not feel comfort with the short timeframe.

"School starts soon and it would be best to get settled before the first classes." Caleb knew that Tom was already missing Rayne.

"I guess the deal is done then." Tom ended the conversation. He saw Caleb to the door without letting him say goodbye to Rayne. Tom was hurt and this was how the hurt was showing. He knew his daughter would not stay at home forever, but this was too sudden for him.

In the morning Tom stated that he and Janie would be using their next vacation time to visit Rayne. Janie mentioned how she was looking forward to going somewhere new. Tom was sullen and Rayne tried to console him.

Over the next few days Tom was settling into the idea that his daughter would be leaving. Rayne packed every day and completed her registration. Caleb's family had gone ahead without him. He and Selena would follow later with Rayne.

It was two days before they were to leave when Rayne started to feel uneasy. There were crows lined up outside her window, and as she looked down she saw there was a coyote sitting by her fence. She grabbed her keys and drove to where Caleb and Selena were staying. It was dawn and the sun was breaking through the thick forest. The crows were above her and the coyote stood beside her. As she made her way closer to the campsite, the pit of her stomach ached. She knew something was wrong.

She crept through the path to the entrance. That was where she saw Caleb and Selena laying on the ground. There was blood but Rayne could not tell where it was coming from. They were not moving. It was a dismal sight as both of them lay side by side. Rayne's eyes pooled with tears. She dropped down to check for a pulse and to hear if they were breathing. Just as she put her head down, Caleb coughed. Rayne was startled. "Caleb wait here. I'm going for help."

Rayne ran through the woods to get a signal for her phone. There was never service at the camp. She dialed 911as she ran toward the ranger station and finally reached an emergency operator as she approached the entrance to the station.

It took less than ten minutes for emergency crews to reach Caleb and Selena. As they got the report from Rayne, they loaded up the two into the ambulance. Caleb had a decent pulse, but they were worried about Selena. She was shot twice in the stomach and they were trying to stop the bleeding. Rayne followed them to the hospital and called her mom when she got there.

Caleb was conscience when she got to see him in his room. He had one gunshot to the stomach and was grazed in the arm. There was a police officer taking his report before Rayne could enter the room. Caleb was vague with what he told the police officer. He said he did not see who did it, that he and his sister were surprised by the attack.

Caleb did not know how bad Selena was. Rayne did not want to tell him. She held his hand as she sat next to him. The room was quiet while they sat together. The only sound was the beeps and clangs from the machines and the chatter from the doctors and nurses outside the door.

That was when she heard Caleb in her head. "I can't hear Selena. How is she?" Rayne did not know what to do or say. She tried not to think for fear that he could hear her.

"I'm not sure. They haven't told me." Again she was telling a half truth.

"They were the people from the other night. The ones that were shooting at us. They came back. I'm only grateful that my family had already left the camp. Rayne we have to go to my family. They can help heal Selena and me." Caleb was in her head.

Suddenly Caleb's thoughts stopped. He waited a minute then spoke to Rayne. "Selena is okay. She is in a lot of pain but she is alive." Just after he had said that a nurse came into the room to tell them Selena was stable now. Once the nurse left the room the doctor came in. The doctor told Caleb about the damage to both he and his sister and how long the two would have to stay in the hospital. Caleb did not say anything but he knew they would not be there as long as the doctor suggested.

Rayne went out to the waiting room while Caleb finished his conversation with the doctor. Her parents were there "How are they?" Both were genuinely concerned.

"Caleb is doing well and Selena is stable." Rayne sat next to her mom.

"Did Caleb say what happened?" Her dad always liked to get to the bottom of things quickly.

"It was a surprise attack. Someone just came into their camp shooting." Rayne spoke in an even tone.

"Oh my Rayne. What if you were there? Would we be out here waiting to hear about you?" Janie had an unnecessary habit of plugging Rayne into a situation and looking at it in a bad perspective.

"Mom it could happen to anyone anywhere. It could happen in our front yard. You never know what people will do these days." Rayne knew she had to keep her parents calm about this or they would fight her about going off to Arizona.

"She's right Janie." Tom sounded defeated when he spoke.

Rayne was surprised to get support from her father on this. Usually it was her mom on her side.

"I'm going back in with Caleb." Rayne got up to leave and her parents asked her to tell Caleb they were praying for them. She smiled a sincere smile to them as she left the room.

The doctor was gone when she went back in with Caleb. Caleb lit up when he saw her. He did not say anything or think anything, but there was something different that Rayne could sense. She felt what he could feel for her. She was warm and it was as if his arms were wrapped around her. She smiled back at him. "I just came to check on you before I go in to see Selena. Will you be okay if I go?"

"Yes go please. She is asking about you."

When Rayne entered Selena's room, she could see that she was hooked to nearly every machine in the room. She was not conscious yet and just like Caleb's room, there were beeps, clangs and drips. A nurse was looking at her chart then glanced a look of reassuring comfort to Rayne. She sat next to Selena when the nurse left the room. In her head she asked "Can you hear me?"

Selena responded "I'm here. How does Caleb look?" They sat in quiet while sending thoughts to each other. By the time Rayne was ready to go back to Caleb, the nurse had come back into the room and noted the marked improvement Selena had made during Rayne's short visit.

Rayne went back to Caleb until visiting hours were over. Caleb told her to check on Selena one more time before she left and reminded her to get her rest so they could leave soon. Rayne did not think they would be leaving the hospital as soon and Caleb suggested, but she told him she would rest.

Selena's pulse was much stronger now and she did not need assistance with breathing anymore. Rayne was confident that the next time she came to see them, Selena would be sitting up in her bed.

Rayne went home and slept heavy that night.

Chapter 33

Remarkable Recovery

It was less than 24 hours since the attack and both Caleb and Selena were up and walking. The doctors could not believe the miracle. They wanted to do tests on the two, but since he had not been to the hospital since his birth, Caleb refused. Because of concern for what the test results might reveal, he wanted to leave. His plans for going to Arizona were still on, and the sooner he and his sister got out of the hospital, the sooner they could leave.

Later that day, a male nurse was found dead near a janitorial closet. It appeared he had a heart attack or possibly an embolism. He was older and had a history of heart disease. The one thing that was in question was where he was found. He was laying wedged in the janitors door, on the children's ward. He was an emergency room nurse and had no need to be on the pediatric floor. It was never reported to the hospital that the nurse was a child predator.

It was during the chaos of the dead nurse when Selena and Caleb snuck out of the hospital. When Rayne went to visit them, they were not in their room. Just as Rayne was leaving, she heard a report at the nurse's station that they were missing.

Rayne left the hospital and went to their old camp. She got out of her car and before she got on the path to walk back, there was a coyote that stepped out to block her. She knew it was warning her not to enter. She was getting better at understanding them. The crows above her started to caw as an additional warning. She was getting used to this form of communication. She went back to her car and pulled out of the parking area. As she drove she noticed Caleb's van behind her. She was about to pull over when she heard Caleb tell her to keep going.

Rayne drove to her house as Caleb followed her. They got out and Rayne asked him why he left the hospital. "I told you we have to leave. We will heal better with my family and it's obviously not safe here. They found out we didn't die and they are still looking for us. Three of us. That means you too Rayne."

"They won't come for me. They have no idea I was there. They don't know where I live."

Caleb did not want to argue with her. He just wanted her to leave with him.

"Give me a day. My dad still knows I'm going with you. I just have to give them a day to get comfortable with it, after all they think you're still in the hospital. I can't just disappear on them like this."

Caleb agreed and he and Selena decided to stay in a hotel for the night. During dinner Rayne told her parents Caleb and his sister were out of the hospital and that they were still on for leaving the next day.

Both parents were surprised that they were healthy enough to travel. Rayne told them she was surprised as well. Caleb would be driving his bus and Selena and Rayne would follow in her car. Her dad reminded her to check her tires, oil and water before they left. Rayne did not understand why her parents made it so easy to go but she did not question it.

Rayne had already had her bags packed earlier that week so she would be ready to leave with Caleb. The next morning Rayne's mom gave her a folder with all of the documents that she would need to get settled into school. Her dad gave her three hundred in cash and a bank card she would be able to use whenever she needed but he warned her not to abuse it. They all shed tears when they hugged goodbye.

Selena volunteered to drive the first round because she knew Rayne would be upset leaving her parents. Tom agreed and was grateful that Selena offered. Rayne waved as they drove off and her parents waved back.

Janie and Tom did not say anything when they got inside their house. Rayne did not say much for the first twenty miles. Selena did not mind, she was not much of a talker. Rayne text her parents a few times before the hum of the road had lulled her into feeling better.

When the sun dropped below the horizon, the three stopped at a stagnated little town to have dinner. Needles California was quiet and slow with just the right amount of traffic running through it to catch a bad soul. Selena had taken the soul of the nurse at the hospital. She needed it in order to heal quickly. Caleb did not want to alert suspicion so he held out for the right moment, fortunately he had enough strength to wait. This town was just what he needed.

They went to a restaurant that boasted its forty years of great service and the best chicken fried steak in town. There were a few big rigs parked alongside it and plenty of areas dark enough to cloak his attack.

Dinner was done and the girls stayed in to pay the tab. Outside, Caleb stood in wait. He scanned across the windows of the rigs to see if he could see a glow. Things were quiet, while most of the truckers were either inside eating or staying the night at the local motels. Caleb remembered seeing a few souls inside the restaurant he could take but it was too risky. He would wait with hopes that one would leave soon.

He sat in the shadow along the building and before he could get comfortable a man shining in a red glow emerged. He had lit up a cigarette and headed toward his truck. He was looking at his cell phone while he was smoking and paying no attention to what was around him. Although he hated cigarette smoke, this was perfect person for Caleb and he took advantage of the timing. Caleb lurched along in the dark and waited for the man to go between the truck trailers. Caleb crawled under one trailer and squat-walked toward where the man was standing. Just as the man was taking what would be his last drag on a cigarette, Caleb attacked. As usual, it took less than 30 seconds to drain the man of his life.

Caleb nearly choked on the smoke from the cigarette. That's when a random thought popped into Caleb's head, "If I didn't take, you those nasty cigarettes would've soon enough".

Just as he was walking out from between the trucks, another trucker was walking back. "Hey there." The trucker solicited acknowledgment, but Caleb kept walking. He sped up and jumped into the seat of his bus. He spoke inside Selena's head to follow close behind him. They were out of the parking lot before the trucker could see what they were driving. They got on the highway and stopped one more time for gas before they were at the site where his family lived.

Rayne called her mom as they pulled in, and by the time she was off the phone, his family was there to greet them. There was a sense of relief that they had made it. Rayne could feel the uneasy thoughts coming from Caleb and Selena, although they had been trying to hide it.

They all settled in for the night and prepared to wake up early.

Chapter 34

Unsettling Information

While Rayne was gone, her dad worked to try to get answers on who had shot Caleb and

Selena. He felt bad for the kids but more so, he was concerned for his daughter and her

safety. Tom knew his daughter was grown and from what he knew, Caleb had a good

family. However, he was indifferent about his vibe with what had been going on lately.

The first call he made was to the officer that he spoke to on the night his wife was

attacked. The officer recalled the incident and reiterated about the recent occurrences

being similar in nature. The three people on the Ortega Highway suffered the same

internal injuries in their deaths. Tom mentioned that he recalled that but wanted to know

if there had been any leads, and if there was any information about the kids getting shot.

The officer told him in confidence, that the lawyer was being investigated for human

trafficking and the officer that died with her was her accomplice. The third person that

had died was one of her clients and they were affiliated with a bad ring of people. The

investigation on the kids was still pending but they had disappeared so they have no one

to question.

Tom thanked the officer for his time and excused himself. Tom had no idea that the kids were not discharged, but in fact they disappeared. He was under the impression that everything was copasetic and Caleb and Selena were cleared to go. Tom called Rayne and woke her up early. He questioned her after he had asked if she was okay. She was emphatic when she told him everything was okay. She told him the only reason they left without checking out was because they had no insurance and the family could not help them. She apologized for the ill behavior. Tom felt better after he hung up with Rayne, but was not going to leave the situation hanging and intended to punish whoever shot the kids.

For the next week, he made it his mission to turn over every rock and piece it together. He used all his resources and collected on all of his favors. He tried to research Caleb and his family but there were no records or paper trail. While there was no record of them staying anywhere in the area, the school district did have information on some transient students that stayed in a campsite on the Ortega Highway. Tom went to the ranger station on the Ortega to see if they could offer anything.

The ranger station was one of many in the Cleveland National forest and fortunately it was the one with information on a family that had set up camp for nearly two years, but just recently moved away. They were quiet, clean, and kept to themselves. There were never any complaints about them, and in fact, they helped to keep the area tidy and maintained.

The only conclusion Tom managed to come to so far, was they were probably a family ashamed of their minimalist lifestyle, which is why they were so elusive. His findings made him feel sympathy for Caleb and Selena. Now more than ever he wanted to help them.

That night Tom fell asleep quickly. He was exhausted from his work, trying not to worry about his daughter.

Although his sleep came quickly, it was interrupted with strange dreams. He dreamt of the night his daughter saved Janie from the stranger. The dream crossed over to the night Caleb's family helped Rayne when she was deathly ill. Finally the dream ended with the sound of humming, and a man speaking to him kindly. They were walking through a dense forest and ended up on a mountain edge. Tom could not see the man he was walking with but his voice soothed him.

Tom was told that his daughter was a great blessing and would do good things in life. He told Tom that he never need worry for his daughter because she would be protected by a higher power. In his dream, he was smiling out into the sunrise. Just as he was smiling in his dream, his alarm clock woke him up. He was still smiling when he sat up.

At breakfast Janie told Tom she had the weirdest dream. While she cooked breakfast, she had replayed her dream to her husband. He was at a loss for words until his wife turned to look at him. The look on his face was pure shock. "What's wrong Tom?" Janie stopped cooking as she looked at him waiting for an answer.

"Could you see the man's face?" Tom's voice was dry when he spoke.

"No I couldn't, but his voice was so soothing. I didn't want him to leave." Janie smiled thinking about her dream.

"Janie, I had the same exact dream. I mean every detail, exactly the same." Tom looked directly into her eyes so she would know he was telling the truth.

"Tom I don't understand what's happening. Should we worry? Have you talked to Rayne?"

"I did. She's fine. I don't think we need to worry. I don't know why, but I feel everything is going to be okay. I think I need to give up this search. I don't know what I'm going to find, but so far everything I've turned up is that Caleb lives in a very humble family. Unfortunately, whoever shot the kids went deep into hiding and probably will never be found."

Janie walked around the table and kissed her husband's forehead "You're a good man Tom. How am I so lucky?"

"I'm the lucky one." He smiled and the two ate breakfast together feeling better than they had in a long time.

Chapter 35

Rayne's Fate

Rayne's dad had called her early to make sure she was okay. She was awake when Selena

came to get her up. Selena was sent to bring Rayne out to eat breakfast with everyone.

Superior was happy to see her. He had been asleep when they pulled in the night before.

"It's so good to see you my child." He put his arm around Rayne and walked her to her

seat.

Selena and Caleb were still stunned every time they witnessed him do this with Rayne.

No one had ever gotten treatment like this from him. He had always been a kind man, but

he seemed to be doting over Rayne with a kindness they had never seen. The elder ladies

of the family were pleased to see Superior so content with Rayne.

The family spent the rest of the day together. They ate, listened to the pleasant hum of the

people, and shared stories of the past. During the sit-in, Rayne had learned that Caleb's

family history started many centuries ago. They emerged from the Pharos in an effort to

keep balance and peace on earth. While there have always been many faiths and beliefs,

there have also been many evils that hide within the faith of the good. It is Caleb's people

that seek the evil embedded in the faithful. While it would appear to be a curse to be born into this family, it was actually a journey. They are to fulfil their journey to their place in the stars, their Nirvana.

Each have a different journey, but they share the same mission. Some go quickly only taking one soul. Some must roam the earth for centuries to accomplish what they are set forth to do.

Their day of sharing all of the good and the bad they witnessed passed quickly, and when it was time to go to sleep Rayne was exhausted. She felt as if she had roamed the earth herself during the day. Superior sent everyone inside to sleep early because morning would come quickly and there would be much to do.

The whole camp slept peacefully through the night and in the morning woke as the sun was breaking the early horizon. When Rayne emerged from her tent, she was surprised to see many trailers and tents had arrived during the night. There were at least one hundred new trailers filling the spaces around her.

As she stood in awe, one of the elderly ladies came to escort her. Selena and Caleb were already at the fire waiting. They were sitting alongside Superior. Everyone looked at Rayne when she walked up. At least two hundred pairs of eyes were focused on her in silence. She blushed as her knees wobbled from anxiety and she nearly fainted. She had never done well in front of a crowd. Just before she thought her knees would buckle, she heard Superior in her mind. "Don't worry my child you've done nothing wrong. They are all here for you. You are the blessing. You are the gift."

After he had calmed her with that thought, a gap opened up through the people. There was a seat at the end and she was brought to it. There were rows of people around her, but even as they moved aside for her, there was not a sound. Finally as she sat at what appeared to be a throne, a low hum started in the crowd. The people started to hum and smile at her, then one by one they walked by and touched her hands. With every touch she could see the path each one had traveled. She had seen the souls they had taken and the lives that they saved.

By the time Superior touched her hand, she was in tears. So much life, so much pain. Rayne was learning that she understood pain and anger differently than these people. It was with the Superior's touch that she learned the most. One thing she learned was that while she was raised to know compassion and empathy, it was a feeling that would destroy these people. She also learned through Superior's touch just how close to death Caleb came when he breathed in Rayne. While there were a flurry of thoughts and feelings, one of the final thoughts that was passed to Rayne was that Superior's wife was brought to the family the same way Rayne was, by an intentional accident.

It was Caleb's destiny to cross paths with Rayne, just as it was Rayne's destiny to nearly die at the hands of Caleb. Rayne's compassion and empathy had been passed to Caleb through Rayne. With compassion and empathy, comes concern, even for heinous beings.

Empathy can keep a soul stealer from completing his or her journey and move onto their Nirvana. If Rayne could not accept her fate, if she could not take a soul, then Caleb's journey would be incomplete.

After everyone sat, Rayne was escorted to her tent where she ate. After she was fed, she had been given a white dress and white flowered crown to put on. Caleb was taken to his tent as well. As he was done with his meal, he was to put on a green shirt and an ivy leaf crown.

They were both brought out of their tents and led along the waterside, up toward the mountain. The people were lined up leading toward the path at the base of the mountain, and as Rayne and Caleb passed them they all fell in line behind the two. There were many different ethnicities with one common life core, to heal the earth of evil souls.

As they reached the first ridge of the mountain, the sun was nearly set. They were brought into a cave that Rayne did not notice on her last hike with Caleb and Selena. Inside the cave, Superior and Selena were sitting by a fire. Rayne and Caleb were brought to them and were to sit next to them on opposite sides. When the cave was full and the ridge was dark, Superior started to hum. His sound was heard alone for minutes while the fire grew. Rayne could see there were hieroglyphics around them.

The pictures Rayne saw would be the story Superior was about to tell. He stopped and all was silent, but for the crackling of the fire.

"I have roamed the earth for over two centuries. For a time I roamed alone. For a time I roamed with a companion. That companion was my wife. She was born of common blood but her fate was greater than common blood. When by chance, she nearly took my life as she crossed my path, then by fate I nearly took hers. Our service has been to guide you all through your journeys. Just as her journey came to an end nearly a century ago, mine too will be coming to an end. Just as my wife was, Rayne is a gift to both our family and to the world. Her fate is to travel a journey she wasn't born into, but was breathed into. Caleb was born a leader, but a leader can't lead without the strength and guidance of his blessing, his companion, his Wife."

As Superior spoke of Rayne's fate, her skin went pale. Companion, Wife. Rayne was barely eighteen and had no thoughts of being a wife or leading people. She could barely lead herself. In her thoughts she heard Superior again "Don't worry my child." Rayne did not know how to not worry about this.

Superior continued to speak to the people.

"As I pass my strength and knowledge to Caleb and Rayne, I will also pass my life to them. They will be your new Superior. Always trust in their word and their work. Know there are enemies around us, but with these two great leaders you will always be protected. Their union will occur one year after my passing. During that time, you must respect them individually and in unity. As with my leadership, you may not question their authority, but trust in their guidance. It is their fate to lead you and your fate to follow."

After his final word he excused all of the people except Selena, Caleb and Rayne. When it was quiet, Superior spoke again. "Selena is my child from birth. She is the daughter of her mother and me. She has been Caleb's confidant and will be Rayne's as well. You three have endured a harsh journey, and unfortunately, there will be many more trials and tribulations. Selena's gift is her connection to me. She still speaks to her mother and when I'm lifted, she will do the same with me. Selena knows she can never reign as Superior, but she plays a vital role for the two of you and she will always serve you well."

Rayne noticed a soft cot that was stretched out along the cave wall. It was covered with a white wool blanket and thick pillow. Superior did not say another word as he walked to the cot and lay himself on it. As he lay quietly, the fire rose high. There seemed to be a hum that came from the fire. It was a hum that was filled with joy and pain. Emotions swirled around the space while the smoke danced over the fire.

There was a sense of peace, and the flames dropped so low that the fire was nearly embers. Selena stood and walked to her father. She kissed his forehead and placed her crown of flowers over his hands. When she left the cave Caleb stood and did the same, only he placed his crown on Superiors head. After Caleb left, Rayne was compelled to stand. She could hear Superior humming in her head. She walked to him and kissed his cheek, then she lay her crown over his heart.

Her eyes pooled with tears. She was torn between a feeling of sorrow and feeling joy. Superior had lived his journey and was with his wife now. It was a time for celebration, but Rayne felt a mourning for a man that she had barely known. She felt like she had lost a lifelong friend.

Rayne walked out of the cave and looked down the path. It was lined with people holding candles. It was a beautiful sight. The people were humming as Rayne walked past. The air was soft as it whirled around her. When she got to the end of the path, Caleb and Selena were waiting for her. Rayne walked between them as they made their way to the campfire to take their seats.

Not one of them said a word. They did not know what to say. Once they sat, the rest of the people gathered around the fire with them. The remainder of the night they all sat around the fire and absorbed and reflected on the day. The next morning they would complete the ceremony for Superior.

Selena could not hear him anymore. She immediately missed having his voice in her head. While she did not recognize or understand her feeling, it was unpleasant and painfully memorable.

Chapter 36

Goodbye, Hello

The sun broke the horizon with bright orange enthusiasm. The circle of people went into their campers and tents to prepare for the final ceremony. They all emerged wearing azure blue clothes. It was symbolic of the sky to which the soul lifts to. They carried fragrant flowers as they walked to the cave where their spiritual leader lay on a cot.

Inside the cave, Caleb took the handles on one end of the cot, while Rayne and Selena took the handles at the other end of the cot. They lifted and carried his lifeless body past their people and shifted him onto a wooden raft that sat along the shoreline.

The family gathered and set their flowers on top of his body. When the last person rested their flowers on him, Caleb poured rose oil on the bundles of sage and lit a single bundle from the fire that Superior would sit at. He took the burning sage and ignited the raft, then the three of them pushed it off into the lake.

It was quiet as they all listened to the crackle of the burning raft. The smoke from the fire wafted into the sky. It danced as it lifted to the perfectly clear blue abyss. While the smoke rose, Caleb started to hum. For her first time, Rayne hummed and the rest of the family joined.

As the raft burned, Selena heard her father's voice. "I am here my child. It is beautiful. Your mother is beautiful." Selena laughed as she cried. She sent a thought to Caleb and Rayne. "I can hear him now." They both looked at her and smiled.

The rest of the day the family joined together to share food and dancing. They were rejoicing in the reunion for their Superior and his wife. They were celebrating their new Superiors, Caleb and Rayne.

Chapter 37

Final Dream

Tom dreamt of the old man again. He saw beauty all around him. He saw Rayne and Caleb. When he saw Rayne, she was glowing white. Tom could see her smiling as she stood next to Caleb.

In his dream the man was guiding Tom through Rayne's night. He had seen what Rayne had seen. He had felt what Rayne had felt. Tom watched the ceremony through Rayne's eyes. He understood the emotions she was working through.

Tom watched as the old man passed peacefully. In his dream Tom understood that his daughter was destined for great things. Although these great things were not the traditional plans Tom had for her, she would do well.

He woke in the morning feeling like he was out of his home. He had to go into his kitchen to make sure of where he was. Janie was already in the kitchen. She was sitting at the table when he walked in. "You had a dream again, didn't you?" Janie knew he had the same dream as her.

"I did. Rayne won't be coming home again will she?" Tom tried not to choke up.

"It was just a dream Tom. I don't know. She'll be fine though, right?" Janie had tears in her eyes.

"She will be fine. There is a plan for her. I know that has to be what the dream is telling us. I know that's what the old man is telling us. I choose to believe that." Tom went to hug his wife. They both cried quietly.

Only minutes of quiet tears passed when a text came through to Tom's phone. It was Rayne. She had text "I miss you guys. Love you. Tell Mom I love her." Tom showed the text to Janie and they both smiled.

"I think everything is going to be fine." Tom kissed Janie's forehead and they cooked breakfast together.

www.ingramcontent.com/pod-product-compliance
Lightning Source LLC
Chambersburg PA
CBHW071132170626
46809CB00002B/585